A SOMEWHAT UNOFFICIAL
INVESTIGATION . . .

Her purring voice laughed. "You must be very dangerous, nobody would ever expect you to be a detective.
How clever of the police to employ you. I am sure
people will tell you anything you want to know!"

She jumped up but held on to his wrist so he was
pulled off the couch. He was in the bathroom before
he knew that she had taken him with her and he saw
her drop her housecoat and step into the tub and adjust
the faucets.

The shower came on. The bath had plastic curtains
but she didn't draw them. He saw the hot water splash
on her shoulders and run down her arms and there
was a small rivulet trickling between her breasts, with
two sidelines running down and causing a steady drip
from her nipples.

"Don't you like to see me like this?"

But he did want to, of course, and he was having
trouble with his breathing. He took her by the hand
before she had had a chance to reach for the towel.

"But I'm still wet."

He pulled the towel off the rack and wrapped it around
her body and swept her off her feet and carried her
through the corridor. . . .

THE BLOND
BABOON

Janwillem van de Wetering

PUBLISHED BY POCKET BOOKS NEW YORK

POCKET BOOKS, a Simon & Schuster division of
GULF & WESTERN CORPORATION
1230 Avenue of the Americas, New York, N.Y. 10020

Copyright © 1978 by Janwillem van de Wetering

Published by arrangement with Houghton Mifflin Company
Library of Congress Catalog Card Number: 77-17338

ISBN: 0-671-82318-3

First Pocket Books printing April, 1979

10 9 8 7 6 5 4 3 2 1

Trademarks registered in the United States and other countries.

Printed in the U.S.A.

To Alexander Stillman

THE BLOND
BABOON

1

"Bit of a breeze," Detective-Adjutant Grijpstra* said.

Detective-Sergeant de Gier agreed with him but he didn't say so. He didn't have to. The pale gray Volkswagen he was trying to steer through the wide, empty thoroughfare of Spui in the center of Amsterdam had just been pushed onto the sidewalk and had stopped, thanks to his timely braking, at about an inch from a lamppost. The engine was still running and he reversed the car, bumping hard on the uneven pavement. The gale, which had started as a deadly suck of cold air, touching the frightened faces of the capital's citizens around lunchtime, had grown to such strength that it could be called a hurricane. It had forced the inhabitants of Holland's flat, below-sea-level coast to go home early, to watch the worrisome weather from behind the plate glass of apartments or the dainty windows of narrow gable houses. They listened to radios and watched TV and noted the State Weather Bureau's forecasts that grew a little more serious as the minutes ticked by. They knew that the authorities had been taken by surprise but that the emergency was being dealt with, and that the dikes were

* The ranks of the Amsterdam municipal police are: constable, constable first class, sergeant, adjutant, inspector, chief inspector, commissaris. An adjutant is a noncommissioned officer.

manned, and that heavy earth-moving machinery was on its way to the danger areas, where high seas were threatening man-made defenses and strengthening their attack methodically, repeating their onslaught every half-minute, raising roaring, foam-topped water mountains in deadly rushes, whipped by shrieking blasts of furious air.

But Sergeant de Gier wasn't concerned with the overall danger of the calamity. He was only trying to do his duty, which, right now, consisted of keeping the Volkswagen moving. He was on normal patrol duty in the city, together with his immediate superior, the large adjutant who was peacefully smoking a small cigar while he held on to the car's roof and commented on the weather.

Grijpstra turned his heavy head, topped by a whitish-gray millimetered bristle, and smiled almost apologetically. "Not too many people around, eh?"

The sergeant, who had got the small car back on the road and was preparing for a U-turn, grunted agreeably.

"They are at home," Grijpstra explained, "where they should be. Maybe they are in bed already, it's nearly eleven. Watch it!"

Grijpstra pointed. De Gier's mouth opened in a soundless shout. An elm, a full-grown tree over forty feet high, was ready to break. They could hear the protesting wood creak and saw the trunk split. De Gier shifted into reverse and pressed the accelerator with his toe. The car began to move, whining. The tree fell ponderously, its foliage touching the round nose of the Volkswagen. Grijpstra sighed.

De Gier was ready to say something but the car's radio had come to life. "Three-fourteen," the radio said politely. "Three-fourteen, come in."

"Go on driving," Grijpstra said. "There are other trees." He had grabbed the microphone from under the dashboard. "Three-fourteen."

"A little job for you, adjutant," the well-modulated voice of a female constable in the radio room of Amsterdam's police headquarters said. "A car of the uniformed police is asking for assistance. They are in the Kalverstraat. Where are you, three-fourteen?"

"Spui."

"Good, you are close. A lot of store windows in the Kalverstraat are smashed by garbage cans. A thief had a go at a jeweler's display and was seen but got away. A small fellow, a little over five feet, long black hair, short new leather jacket. In his late twenties. The colleagues think he is still close by."

"Right," Grijpstra said without any enthusiasm. "We'll join the chase on foot so that we can see what is falling on us."

"Good luck, adjutant. Out."

Grijpstra was still clambering out of the Volkswagen when de Gier sprinted away, leaning over to counterbalance the gale's driving force. Grijpstra cursed gently as he moved his bulk into motion. The athletic sergeant was waiting for him on the sidewalk, sheltered behind a parked truck.

"Which way?" de Gier asked. Grijpstra pointed as he ran.

"Let's try the alleys."

De Gier jumped ahead, veering toward the protected side of a side street while the wind howled along storefronts, pulling at signboards and gutters. A lid of a garbage can obstructed his way and he jumped and shouted a warning, but the adjutant had seen it and kicked the rolling disc so that it shot off at a tangent. A few cardboard boxes followed the lid and the policemen avoided them, turning into a passage that would take them to the main shopping center of the Kalverstraat. Grijpstra stopped running.

"In here somewhere," he panted. "He is bound to be somewhere around here. In the Kalverstraat he can be seen—the stores all have glass porches. Let's go."

"Wait," de Gier said softly and put out a restraining hand.

"What?"

"I think I saw a head pop out, over there. I'll go."

Grijpstra grinned as he watched the sergeant's progress.

De Gier was sliding with slow, exaggerated movements. His tall slim shape merged with the alley's shadows. The hunter, the deadly hunter. But Grijpstra stopped grinning. He was sure that de Gier would make his kill. Ferocious, he thought. Very.

As de Gier jumped ahead and flattened himself against the aged, crumbling front of a small house, Grijpstra stepped back and drew out his heavy service pistol, loading it as he jerked it out of its cracked holster. He shook his head. There had been times, not so long ago, that he wouldn't have thought of drawing his gun, but thieves were changing. Hit-and-run thieves were usually armed these days, with knives mostly, with firearms occasionally if they were desperate enough, because the drug habit was forcing them to be desperate. He covered the slow-moving sergeant, edging inch by inch along his wall. The sergeant reached the porch and froze. There was no movement for a little while. The gale seemed to have the alley to itself, wheezing up strength while it rattled windows and doors tentatively. The thief would show himself again. The thief was in there. The thief was nervous. The thief wanted to know what was happening.

Out popped the head. Long shiny black hair framing a furtive eye peeping over the turned-up collar of a leather jacket. The sergeant's hand shot out and grabbed the head by the hair and pulled. The thief tumbled from the porch. A plastic bag dropped and clanged as it hit the pavement's gleaming bricks. A knife flashed.

"*Police*," Grijpstra roared. The knife fell too. The sergeant's thumb had found the thief's wrist and had pressed it cruelly while his fingers twisted. The thief squeaked.

"Handcuffs," de Gier said, and Grijpstra put his gun back and produced the required article. The cuffs clicked. De Gier blew his whistle. The shrill earsplitting sound cut through the gale's roar. Two uniformed constables came running into the alley.

"Ha!" the constables shouted. "Got him!"

"Got him," de Gier said. "Here you are, with the compliments of your CID.* Why didn't you catch him your-

* Criminal Investigation Department.

selves? We're supposed to drive about quietly and not to interfere.''

"We are old men," the constable facing de Gier said, "and we like to give others a chance. Nasty wind, what?"

"Bit of a breeze," Grijpstra agreed. "You don't mind if we go back to our car, do you? If it is still there—an elm nearly got it just now. Did you see this man break in?"

"I didn't break in," the thief said. "The window was all broken and the stuff was spilling out into the street so I picked it up to take it to a police station, but these fools were running and firing their guns so I ran too. I don't want to get killed."

Grijpstra patted the narrow leather shoulder. "Professional, are we?"

The thief looked up. His eyes had widened with fear and he shivered.

"We'll take him. You want your handcuffs back, adjutant?"

"Of course, constable. My private property, I saved up for them."

The cuffs were taken off and the constable brought out another pair. The thief looked unhappy. "Ouch! Too tight!"

"They are not too tight," the constable said, tugging the steel grips gently. "See? Plenty of room. We'll take them off at the station. Come along."

"Home," de Gier said as he twisted his tall body into the Volkswagen's driving seat. "The wind will be hitting my balcony full on. It'll be tearing up my plants and Tabriz will be nervous. She'll be at the marmalade jar again."

"Marmalade jar?" Grijpstra asked. "What does a cat want with a marmalade jar?"

"Throw it on the floor and break it, what else? So that I can cut my feet and then slither about in the jelly—it has happened twice already. The last time I fell on the table and tried to steady myself on a shelf and I broke just about everything in the kitchen and cut an artery in my ankle."

"I know." The adjutant tried to stretch but gave up the attempt. His shoulder hurt; he had probably bumped it during the chase. "You took a week off, remember? But I still want to know why a cat gets at a marmalade jar."

There were more trees down, and de Gier was maneuvering around their fallen twisted forms. One of the windows of the car didn't close and the wind cried through it, a high-pitched evil wheeze. "They used to have that sound on radio plays. Horrible sound. I would always switch off the program. To accompany young girls raped in attics, as if the crying and sobbing weren't enough."

"Cat," Grijpstra said. "Marmalade jar."

"I don't know why she does it, a way to show her displeasure, I suppose. Cats have their ways. Your household will be a mess too, with your wife and kids rattling all through the place."

Grijpstra frowned. "My wife won't rattle. She'll ooze. She got fatter again, you know, I didn't think she would do it but she did. She's sleeping on the floor now, bed won't hold her weight." He took the microphone out of its clasp.

"Headquarters, Three-fourteen."

"Come in, Three-fourteen."

"We caught your thief and gave him to the constables and we are on our way to the garage."

There was a strange breaking noise and Grijpstra stared at the microphone, which looked small and innocent in his large hand.

"Window got blown in," the female constable said. "That's the second window tonight. It's a mess here. My notebook has blown away. Did you say you are coming back?"

"Yes, we were supposed to go off duty at eleven. It's close to midnight now."

"I *am* sorry, but I have another assignment for you. We're short of staff again—everybody is out helping people who got trapped, there are crushed cars all over the city, and we're having panic calls from people who got their walls blown in or roofs torn off. And people have been blown into the canals and, oh, all sorts of things."

"Is that the sort of job you have for us?" Grijpstra asked,

dangling the microphone as if it were a dead mouse.

She tried to laugh. "No, adjutant, the uniformed police and the fire department are around too. I have a proper job for you, a dead lady. A health officer called just now. He was supposed to pick up a corpse, but the doctor hasn't come and the death isn't natural anyway. An accident, according to the lady's daughter. Lady fell down the garden stairs and broke her neck. The ambulance can't take the corpse until they have clearance from us. Mierisstraat Fifty-three. Just a routine call, probably."

Grijpstra showed his teeth. The microphone was still dangling.

"Three-fourteen?"

De Gier stopped the car and tugged the microphone from Grijpstra's hand.

"We'll go, dear. Do you have any additional information? The Mierisstraat is a nice quiet little street. Nobody throws anybody down the stairs of a house in the Mierisstraat."

'That's all I know, sergeant. Dead lady, fell down the garden stairs and presumably broke her neck. The health officer says she is dead."

"Okay."

"Out."

De Gier pulled a knob on the dashboard and a small pale red light came on as the siren began to howl from its hiding place under the hood. Grijpstra lifted the blue sparkle light from the glove compartment and rolled his window down. The magnet clicked the light onto the car's thin roof and its reflection lit up the wet street surface around them, sweeping a ghostly wide beam on the reflecting road. The Volkswagen shot away as de Gier's foot came down. The gale grabbed the car at the next corner and pushed it to the middle of the glimmering tar. It was raining hard suddenly and the wipers had trouble keeping the windshield clear. A streetcar approached from the opposite direction and de Gier twisted the wheel viciously. The streetcar's bell was clanging as its long yellow shape flashed past. Grijpstra closed his eyes and groaned. The driving rain became a solid white spray in the headlights, then it stopped. Another streetcar threw up a sheet of gray liquid dirt that hit the Volkswagen head on. De Gier cursed and braked. The windshield wipers cut through the mud and he could see again. The car skidded around a tree, a huge poplar that had fallen parallel to the sidewalk. A branch got into the right front wheel and wrapped itself around the tire. De Gier drove on and they could hear twigs snap. Grijpstra opened his eyes.

De Gier was laughing. "Look! We're driving through a forest."

The poplar's leaves were brushing Grijpstra's windows.

"That lady was probably blown down her stairs," he said morosely, "and that fool health officer shouldn't have phoned. Doesn't he know we're busy tonight?" He closed his eyes again. The wind was pushing the car toward a canal and the Volkswagen was skidding. The sergeant pumped the brake and steered with the skid. They stopped a few feet from the rail, a thin rail, about a foot high, meant to stop parked cars from sliding into the water.

"We're all right," de Gier said and reversed. The wind was whipping at the car's rear and they were gathering speed.

The adjutant kept his eyes closed. It'll happen again, he thought, remembering how he had been in a small car that slipped into a canal and sank slowly and nearly drowned him; he had been saved in the nick of time by a fire brigade's crane. He badly wanted to shout at de Gier, to tell him that the lady was dead, and that they wouldn't revive her by hitting a tree or drowning in a muddy canal or getting under a streetcar. He wanted to ask the sergeant why he had switched the siren on if the din of the gale was so overwhelming that they had hardly been able to hear the streetcar's electric bell clamoring right next to their ears.

Grijpstra opened his eyes when de Gier's hand brushed past him. The sergeant was switching off the siren. They had arrived. Mierisstraat. He recognized it. Quiet, slightly elegant. Wide sidewalks lined with tall plane trees. Tall narrow houses, turn of the century. A street of doctors and lawyers and comfortable upper-middle-class families making their money in gentle leisurely ways. An unlikely street to be stalked by violent death. A street where pedigreed dogs lift their legs daintily before they spray a lamppost. He smiled. The smile didn't come to full bloom.

"Dog," Grijpstra said, and his fist hit de Gier's side softly.

"Dog, damn it. Same address. Day before yesterday. Cardozo was supposed to take care of the complaint. Remember?" De Gier whistled.

"Same address. Poisoned dog. Mierisstraat Fifty-three. Cardozo didn't want to go."

"Right." De Gier's handsome profile was nodding solemnly.

"You had to kick him out of the room. And he was talking about it yesterday. He had a suspect, he said. Man who lives in the rear. The gardens meet. He had some of the dog's puke in a bottle. Very proud of himself. Lab test proved arsenic poisoning."

While de Gier's head nodded Grijpstra's head shook. "Bad. A poisoned dog and a lady with a broken neck. Same address. We'll be busy."

They waited while they thought. Police reasoning. Something small happens, then something big happens. Same place. There would be a connection. They waited until a respectful gloved hand tapped on the windshield.

De Gier got out and the health officer saluted.

"Evening, sergeant. Haven't met for a while, have we? Different routes. My mate is waiting for you inside. The lady's daughter is a bit upset, he is keeping her quiet. The two ladies live by themselves, no man in the house. And there is something with a dog. Poisoned, so the young lady says."

"The wind," Grijpstra said hopefully, "the bloody gale. Sure the gale didn't grab your lady?"

"No, adjutant." The health officer's face showed helpfulness and apology neatly blended. "The gale can't reach into the gardens here. The houses are high, you see. The wind may be getting at the tops of the trees but it can't reach down to the garden stairs. I've been out in the garden awhile, nice and quiet. But maybe she slipped. It had been raining earlier on and the stairs are wet and she was wearing high-heeled shoes and a long dress."

"A party?"

"Could be. There's a smell of alcohol and an empty bottle. The daughter says there was no party. Lady liked to drink by herself."

"Wasn't she with her mother when it happened?"

"No. The young lady has her own apartment, top floor. She said she came down to check if everything was all right before going to bed. The garden door was open and her mother . . . Well, you'll see."

De Gier was looking at the closed door. A good-quality door with simple dignified ornamentation. Varnished oak with a garland of leaves. Two nameplates and two bells. Elaine Carnet. Gabrielle Carnet. Hand-painted nameplates, white on green. Polished brass bells. A polished brass knocker in the shape of a lion's head.

The door moved as his hand reached for the lower bell.

This is a bad night, de Gier thought, and he waited for the door to open altogether. A very bad night. I should be home to safeguard the balcony's plants and to comfort Tabriz and to have a hot shower and several mugs of strong tea. It wouldn't be a bad night if I were home. But I am not, and this is a killing.

He couldn't be sure, of course, but he was. As sure as Grijpstra, who was standing just behind him. Each profession develops its devotees. The detectives of Amsterdam's murder brigade are trained to be suspicious, but that doesn't mean much more than that they are always suspicious. They ask mild questions and they look at faces and dig about in the endless chain of cause and event, but their eyes are quiet and their voices soft and their manners mild. Not always. There are moments when the detectives quiver, when little fiery stabs touch their spines, when they sweat slightly, and when their eyes open and stare fiercely.

Gabrielle Carnet stepped back quickly and nearly stumbled. De Gier's long arm shot out and steadied her.

"Evening, miss," he said, forcing himself to keep his voice down to the prescribed level of politeness. "We are the police."

Grijpstra had walked past the sergeant. He followed the other health officer through a long corridor, a central hall, into an enclosed porch, to the garden door.

Elaine Carnet, a soaked sad shape, lay crumpled at the bottom of the steps. The health officer pulled the blanket away. The head had snapped back at a most unnatural angle. The woman's dead eyes stared out of a messy arrangement of sodden make-up smears. Her double chin was stretched tight by the position of the head. The hair, neatly puffed up into fluffy curls only a few hours before, clung to the wet scalp. The wide mouth was smiling, and the gold fillings of two canines sparkled in the light filtering from the porch windows. The smile seemed genuine, a joyous surrender to an unexpected but welcome visitor.

Grijpstra stepped over the corpse and squatted. The light fell differently now and the smile had become a snarl. The sudden change upset him and he went back to the steps. A smile again, definitely.

It was only later that he remembered a common feature of the two facial expressions. The common denominator was victory. Something had pleased Elaine Carnet, some event had elated her seconds before she died. The thought sparkled through his brain but didn't ripen just then. He had already settled down in his routine. He was observing his surroundings.

"Leave her here?" the health officer asked.

"Sure. I'll get the experts. We want some photographs."

There was a phone on the porch and he dialed. "Commissaris?"

"Yes," a soft voice answered.

"I know you are ill, sir, but I thought I would phone you all the same. We've run into something, Mierisstraat Fifty-three. It's a bad night, sir. Shall I phone the inspector?"

"No. I'm feeling better. Send de Gier to fetch me— there's a tree blocking my garage and there won't be any taxis tonight. What have you got, adjutant?"

"A poisoned dog, sir, and a dead lady." Grijpstra moved to the window and looked out. Big raindrops were clattering down on the corpse. "A very dead lady, sir."

2

"Miss?" de Gier asked as he steadied the girl. "Are you all right?"

"Yes. Gabrielle, that's my name, Gabrielle Carnet. You are the police?"

He showed his card but she wasn't interested. She looked at it, and he put it back into the breast pocket of his tailored denim jacket. The rain had gotten into his silk scarf, and he pulled it free and refolded it before tucking it back into his open shirt. The scarf was a very light shade of blue. The denim jacket and the matching tight trousers were dark blue. She followed his movements dreamily. Her eyes came up to his face, noting the full brushed-up mustache and the high cheekbones and the large glowing brown eyes.

"Are you really a policeman?"

"Yes. I showed you my card just now. Detective-Sergeant de Gier. Rinus de Gier. We answered the health officer's call. Was it you who phoned the ambulance service?"

"Yes." Her voice was low. It had an interesting quality. He tried to determine what it was. Silky? No. Something with texture. Velvety. A purring voice. The voice she would use on men, not on women. She would have a different voice for women.

"What happened, miss? Would you tell me, please?"

She still seemed unsteady on her legs, and he looked around for a place to sit down. The corridor was bare except for a carpet and a small table next to the coat rack. He put a hand under her elbow and guided her to the stairs.

"Sit down, miss. You'll feel better."

He automatically noted her particulars. Small, five foot perhaps, a little over, but that was due to the high heels of her stylish soft leather boots. Dungarees tucked into the boots. Tight dungarees hiding slightly bowed legs. A very short blouse that showed skin at both ends. A narrow waist with a little bellybutton and the shine of a gold chain. A fashionable girl. The blouse's top button was open, he could see the curve of her breasts. Long, dark brown hair, glossy. No jewelry. A pointed small face, uninteresting if it hadn't been for the eyes, but the eyes were cleverly made up, they weren't as large as they seemed. The color was startling, a shiny green. Metallic bright eyes. The possibility of drugs immediately presented itself but he could see her arms. No pricks. Perhaps she sniffed cocaine or took pills. But the feverish shine of her eyes could be just due to anguish. The young lady's mother had died.

When she began to speak he noticed the purr again. It couldn't be natural. She was acting, showing off, so the shock of her mother's death had already worn thin. She had taken time to adjust her make-up. The thin penciled lines around the eyes weren't ten minutes old.

"I live upstairs," Gabrielle Carnet was saying, "in my own apartment. Mother and I split up last year. The house was remodeled. My apartment is self-contained."

"Can you hear your mother's doorbell, miss?"

"Not when I am in my kitchen or bathroom."

"Do you know whether your mother had a visitor?"

"I don't know." She sobbed in between the words and her hands twitched. Her hair had fallen over her eyes and she pushed it away, smearing the mascara. A genuine reaction. But genuine about what? Was she sorry she pushed or kicked her mother down the stairs?

"Go on," he said gently, trying to tune his voice and

mood to hers.

"I came down about an hour ago, I always check before I go to sleep. Mother drinks a bit and sometimes she falls asleep in front of the TV and I have to wake her up and take her upstairs."

"I am sorry, I have to ask questions. You know that, don't you, Miss Carnet?" She nodded. She was trying to get a handkerchief from her pocket but it stuck and she got up. He got up too. "Do you want to go upstairs, miss?"

"No. It's all right here."

They sat down again. She was sitting very close; he could feel the warmth of her thigh.

"Was your mother an alcoholic, miss?"

"Yes. No."

"How much did she drink, a day, I mean. Did she drink every day?"

"Most days, but only wine. Good wine. A bottle a day perhaps, but I think she was drinking more lately. I didn't see very much of her anymore, we were living separately."

"Because of some trouble? Did you fight?" He kept his voice as low as he could to take the sting out of the key words. Alcoholic. Fight. They weren't good words but he had to use them.

"No, we didn't fight, we just didn't get on. I'm nearly thirty now. I should have a place of my own but I didn't want to live somewhere else, she needed care. Oh, my God."

She was crying and he waited. Her thigh was still pressing against him. He didn't like the girl, but why didn't he? She wasn't pretty but she was certainly attractive. An attractive pushover. He could hear Grijpstra's booming voice dominating the health officers farther down the house. If they weren't around he could make the girl right on the stairs, dead mother or no dead mother. He could feel his lips stretching into a sneer. A most unbecoming thought. A policeman is a public servant. But the fact was that the girl wakened nothing in him, nothing at all. And he was sure she was lying. Gabrielle should have heard her mother scream as she fell down the stairs. But there was the gale.

Perhaps its noise had drowned the scream. The gale seemed to have found the street at that very moment, and he could hear its deep, menacing, sonorous whoosh and the rattle of parked cars being pushed into each other.

"Sergeant?"

De Gier looked up. "Yes, Grijpstra?"

"Would you go and fetch the commissaris? I phoned the experts, they'll come down as soon as they get their gear together. The doctor is on his way too."

"Sure."

"And get Cardozo too if you can. He's off duty tonight, he's visiting friends, but his mother gave me the address, it's on the way. He knows you're coming."

The girl was still crying and hiding her face. Grijpstra's eyebrows arched. De Gier shook his head silently. His mouth formed the word "lying." Grijpstra nodded. De Gier got up and gestured invitingly. Grijpstra lowered his body slowly. The girl felt his bulk on the step and edged away.

"You can tell me what you told the sergeant, miss. Do you know what happened?"

The front door clicked behind de Gier. The health officers came and said good-bye. Grijpstra could hear the engines of the Volkswagen and the ambulance start as the gale breathed in for a second only to roar away at full strength.

"Miss?"

"She must have fallen down the stairs," Gabrielle said. "I think she worried about her azaleas and opened the garden door, and then the wind pulled the door out of her hands and she lost her balance."

"Come with me, miss, please."

He pulled her to her feet and she followed him down the corridor and into the large sitting room. He glanced at the room's wall. A bookcase holding a beautifully bound encyclopedia, brand-new and never used. A row of artbooks, just as new. A flower arrangement. A modern painting. There was a thick wall-to-wall carpet under his feet, off-white to set off the darker furniture. A showroom designed by an interior decorator. The porch was more personal, with a battered old TV on a cane table and some easy chairs that looked ugly and comfortable.

"Your mother liked to sit on the porch, miss?"

"Yes. She had it glassed in when she moved here, some ten years ago, I think. She was always here, it's the only part of the house that wasn't redecorated. And my apartment, of course. I did that myself after the carpenters were done."

Grijpstra had opened the garden door. "There's no wind here, miss. These gardens are well protected. The houses won't let the gale in. See?"

"Yes."

"So how did your mother fall down the stairs?" Grijpstra's voice was kind and puzzled. He looked solid, trustworthy, fatherly. He was very concerned. "Now how could such an awful accident have happened? Your mother knew these stairs well, didn't she? Did she like gardening?"

"Yes."

"She planted those bushes over there, didn't she? Those are nice azaleas. Did she plant the hedge in the back as well?"

"Yes."

Gabrielle wandered around the room dreamily. She reached for the wineglass on a low table near the TV. Grijpstra touched her arm. "Don't touch anything, please, miss. We'll have that glass checked for fingerprints. Is this your mother's ring, miss?" He showed her a smooth gold wedding ring that was lying on a bare board near the garden door. She stooped.

"Don't pick it up please, miss."

"Yes, that's my mother's ring."

"Did she play with it? Put it on and take it off when she was nervous?"

"No."

"Did it fit tightly?"

She was crying, fighting the tears, biting on her handkerchief.

"I'm sorry, miss."

The girl had sat down, and he sat down opposite her and

rubbed his cheeks. He could do with a shave again, there hadn't been much time that morning. His wife had come into the bathroom and he wanted to get away, so he had done a sloppy job. He would do better later on, she would be asleep by then. The thought of scalding hot water soaking into the stubby folds and the neat strokes of a new razor blade cheered him up somewhat. He didn't like cornering the girl. De Gier thought she was lying, and she very likely was. But there could be extenuating circumstances. A drunken, nagging mother, wailing, screaming. A family fight. A push. Most anything can be explained and understood, if not accepted. But if there had been a struggle it would be better for the girl to admit to it, now, when everything was still fresh. It would look better in court. But he wasn't going to feed her a confession. Perhaps the commissaris would. He would wait.

The girl looked up. "I don't want to cry."

"No, miss, I understand. Perhaps we can have some coffee. I'll make it if you tell me where everything is."

"No. I can do it."

He followed her to the kitchen and stood around while she worked. Her movements were organized, efficient. The percolator began to gurgle, then throb. She was staring out at the garden when he began to look for the garbage container. He found it fitted into a cupboard under the sink, attached to the cupboard door. There was another wineglass in the plastic bag protecting the container. The glass had broken at the stem. It was of the same type as the glass he had seen on the table near the TV. He took a long-handled fork lying on the kitchen counter and poked around in the bag. There were several cigar stubs, each stub connected to a plastic mouthpiece, and some cigar ash. The ashtray stood on the counter. It had been cleaned.

A visitor after all. There was no lipstick on the mouthpieces and both Gabrielle and her mother used lipstick. Women smoked cigars these days, and the cigars would have been long and very thin. De Gier sometimes smoked cigars like that; de Gier was vain. A vain male visitor. But who isn't vain?

I am not vain, Grijpstra thought, looking down at his crumpled suit. The suit was made of excellent British material, pure wool, dark blue with a fine white stripe. He was vain enough to buy expensive suits, always of the same type, but he treated them badly. All right, he would admit to some vanity. Still, he wouldn't smoke sissy cigars with imitation mouthpieces. No, perhaps he would. If he could afford them. They would go with his suit. He breathed heavily so that the air burbled past his pressed lips. Nothing was ever easy. Suspects lie and hide their emotions. Clues aren't seen or get lost. De Gier thought the girl was lying and he was following the sergeant, but why should he? The sergeant's impressions were sieved through the sergeant's own perceptions, forced into shapes, twisted out of truth perhaps.

A man visits Elaine Carnet. Elaine is all dressed up in a long flowered dress. A summer evening. She had done everything possible to doll herself up. She is a woman and she won't admit to getting old. How old would she be? Early fifties? Yes, most likely. She waits for the man in the intimacy of her porch. She gets up, walks around carefully, her dress rustles. A whiff of perfume pervades the room. The azaleas are blooming behind her. The setting sun touches the tops of the poplars and elms and drooping willows. That's what she had anticipated but instead there is a storm, a horrible oppressive atmosphere that creeps into everything, into her very soul, into the mind of the man. They drink wine together, a strong Beaujolais, and the storm gets into the wine too and turns it into a violent brew that seeps into their thoughts. She talks to him. Her voice is raw and cutting. She talks about the past. She twists off her wedding ring and flings it on the floor. A sudden accusation hurts the man to the quick, and he throws his cigar into the ashtray and jumps up and grabs her by the neck and shakes her. The garden door is open and he sees it and pushes her and lets go. And then he leaves.

The girl's eyes were resting on Grijpstra's face.

"Yes, miss?"

"The coffee is ready. I'll take it to the porch."

"Please, miss."

He sipped the coffee and went through the fabricated scene again. It fitted all the facts. But he wouldn't ask any more questions now. The girl seemed in a steady frame of mind again.

The bell rang and the girl went to open the door. She came back followed by de Gier, who introduced her to the commissaris and Cardozo. Grijpstra got up and offered his chair to the commissaris, who accepted gratefully and lowered his frail body carefully into its rumpled cushions. Cardozo, looking even more boyish and flushed than usual, brought in a chair from the living room and gave it to Grijpstra and went back to fetch stools for de Gier and himself.

"Well, miss. This is a bad business," said the commissaris. "My sergeant has been telling me about it in the car. We are sorry to bother you, but do you feel you are ready to answer some questions? We'll be as quick as we can."

His pale, almost colorless eyes glinted behind the round gold-rimmed spectacles. His thin hands were holding his knees. He looked neat and harmless in his worn but recently pressed three-piece suit. A gold watch chain spanned his slightly protruding stomach, and the perfectly knotted tie and thinning hair combed into two equal halves perfected the image of a kind but exact person of authority, a headmaster, a miniature patriarch even.

"Perhaps you would like some coffee, sir, Miss Carnet has just made some. Excellent coffee."

"That would be very nice but perhaps Miss Carnet shouldn't bother. Cardozo can get it."

Gabrielle got up to show Cardozo the kitchen and the commissaris turned quickly. "Anything of interest, Grijpstra?"

He listened as he was told about the wedding ring, the second wineglass, and the cigar stubs.

"Any theory, adjutant?"

"A visitor, male presumably. An argument. We don't know about Mrs. Carnet's marital status yet."

"You haven't asked?"

"The girl was very nervous, sir. I waited for you."

"Good."

The commissaris's hands moved up and squeezed his thin thighs.

"How are you feeling, sir?"

"It was a bad attack, adjutant, rheumatism in its pure and vilest form, but I think the crisis has passed. The sergeant thought the girl was lying. What do you think?"

"I don't know, sir."

The coffee came. The commissaris talked about the gale. De Gier's car had been the only vehicle on the trip back. Fallen trees and overturned cars everywhere. Capsized trucks even. And the gale still in full force.

"Did you hear the news, sir?"

"Yes, it's bad, but the dikes are holding so far. The army is moving out to help, but we may be flooded by tomorrow. How far are we below sea level here?"

The opinions ranged from ten to thirty feet. The commissaris tittered. He seemed truly amused. The titter loosened the room's murky atmosphere. De Gier laughed and the girl smiled. Cardozo looked surprised and pulled his long curly hair.

"Well. I believe that Detective Constable Cardozo and Miss Carnet have already met. A matter of a poisoned dog. How is your dog now, Miss Carnet?"

It was the right thing to say and the commissaris moved with the girl's welcoming reaction. The dog was upstairs in her apartment and he wanted to see it. The bell rang again.

"That'll be the doctor, or the photographers, perhaps. De Gier, why don't you answer the door. Grijpstra can take charge here, and Cardozo and I will go up with Miss Carnet."

Grijpstra nodded. He had wanted to take the girl upstairs too, to keep her near her mother's corpse was a mistake, she would never talk easily that way, but he had wanted to stay near the front door and to keep the girl in sight at the same time. The commissaris, Cardozo, and the girl were on their way up by the time de Gier let in the photographers and the doctor. The men didn't say much, their usual ribaldry suppressed by the sinister howling of the gale. They all seemed intent to do the job as soon as possible and get away.

"Beautiful, beautiful," the commissaris said as he saw the Oriental rugs, the cushions with simple geometric designs thrown about in charming disorder, the low couch, the modern paintings. A small white terrier, whimpering softly, was trying to get out of its basket. The commissaris bent down and scratched the animal between its pointed ears. "Sick, are we?"

"He's much better now," Gabrielle said softly. "Would you like more coffee? I can make some in my kitchen here."

"Lovely, lovely," the commissaris said, and he sat down on a cushion near the dog's basket. He was still talking to the dog in a low voice. "Feeling better, eh? Somebody gave us some poison, did he? Somebody who isn't right in the head. We'll find him and talk to him."

The dog put out a paw and the commissaris held it. Cardozo had knelt down near the basket too. The dog turned his head and licked the young detective's hand.

"What do you know about this, Cardozo?" the commissaris whispered fiercely.

"Miss Carnet came to see us day before yesterday, sir. I went home with her. The dog was in a bad state, but the vet was taking care of him. Pumped out his stomach. I took a sample and had it tested by the laboratory. It contained arsenic, a big dose. The particulars are in my report."

"Yes? And then?"

"Miss Carnet said that the dog usually plays by himself in the garden when her mother and she are out. They had been out for lunch, and when she came back she found Paul, that's his name, in the kitchen. He seemed very sick, retching and whining, and she called the vet, who came immediately and told her that Paul had been poisoned and that she should go to the police. She took her car and came to see us at once. When I had spoken to the vet I checked the houses that have gardens bordering the Carnet garden, five in all. Everybody seemed sympathetic and upset about the poor dog except the man who owns the house directly behind this one. A man called de Bree, an engineer, fat fellow, bald head, fifty years old, I think.''

"And what did Mr. de Bree say?''

"He didn't say very much, sir. He slammed the door in my face after telling me not to bother him and that he had had nothing to do with the damn dog.''

"Hmm.'' The commissaris still looked fierce. "Ah, there we are. Nice fresh coffee, I can smell it. Just the thing on a horrible night like this.''

Gabrielle smiled. Only one shaded light had been switched on and her small shape blended well with the exotic background of the fairly large room. An Arab princess entertaining important visitors. The commissaris smiled too, the thought had cheered him up. She had gone to great trouble to decorate the room; he wondered what her daydreams were like. She seemed to be living by herself, for there was no trace of a man's presence. A very feminine room. He remembered de Gier's remark about drugs, the sergeant could be right. The commissaris had been in the rooms of junkies often, far too often. Junkies like the Middle and Far East and imitate their, to them, bizarre environment. He had noticed the torn Persian carpets and dirty cushions bought at the flea market, but this room looked both expensive and clean. Junkies are messy, Gabrielle was not. Junkies also like a profusion of plants and any number of trinkets, small objects strewn about. No, this room was different. He saw the neat row of potted house plants on the windowsill and a bookcase filled with paperbacks arranged according to their color.

"Tell me about your mother, Miss Carnet, what was she like?''

Gabrielle didn't respond. She was trying to but no words came, her small hands gestured vaguely.

"Your father?''

The hands balled and then relaxed suddenly. "Mother

was never married. I don't know who my father is. I don't think she knew either, the subject was never mentioned. If I brought it up she would evade my questions, so I gave up."

"I see. Your name is French, isn't it? Carnet, I can't recall ever having heard it before."

"Belgian. Mother was born in Brussels but she lived in Paris for some time. Her father ran away and she had to support herself and her mother. We haven't been very lucky with men in the family."

Her voice was light, conversational. There seemed to be no grudge in it.

"And how did your mother support herself in Paris?"

"She sang. There's a stack of old records downstairs, she was famous once. She sang chansons in nightclubs, just after the war, for a few years. She did very well until she became pregnant."

The commissaris's brain produced a small question but he didn't ask it. There was no point in asking; Gabrielle wouldn't know the answer. Pregnancy can be solved by abortion. An abortion in Paris wouldn't have presented a large problem. Did Elaine Carnet have hopes of marrying the father of her child? There was a wedding ring on the floor of the porch below. Had the father bought the ring or had Elaine Carnet got it herself, later, after she had given up all hope?

"Yes," he said. "And then your mother came to Holland?"

"Yes, my grandmother had friends here but they are dead now, my grandmother is dead too. Mother liked it here, she never left."

"And she sang again?"

"No. She has a business, Carnet and Company. The company sells furniture, Italian furniture mostly. Mother made some good contacts, and she used to be very energetic. She had saved money from her singing and she was looking around for a way to invest it, and then she saw an advertisement of some Italian firm that wanted to have an agent here. The Italians spoke French and Mother spoke

French too, of course, and she went to Milan and got the agency and bought some stock and she was lucky, I think. The firm does very well now. Oh!" The hand had come up suddenly and covered her mouth.

Cardozo jumped up, but the commissaris touched his leg and he sat down again.

"Yes, miss?"

"Mr. Bergen. He will be very upset about Mother. He is her partner, you see. I should have called him."

"Perhaps you should call him tomorrow. With this weather he'll be better off at home. Does Mr. Bergen live in Amsterdam?"

"Yes, but on the other side of the city."

"We shouldn't disturb him then. Did your mother start the business with him?"

"He came in a little later. She started on her own and he was working for another firm selling furniture. I think they met somewhere and she offered him a job on commission and he did well. Later he became a director and a partner; she gave him a quarter of the shares."

"Mr. Bergen is married, is he?"

"Yes."

The commissaris shifted on his cushion. "I am sorry, miss. You don't have to answer the question if you don't want to. Did your mother have any close friends? Men, I mean."

She giggled. Cardozo hunched his shoulders. He had been watching the girl carefully, fascinated by her flowing hair and startling green eyes and firm breasts, but he had reminded himself that he was a police officer and that the girl had just lost her mother, by an accident or otherwise. Her purring voice had set off tiny ripples below the skin of his back. He had been impressed by the room and the way the girl's small body controlled the room. He had had the feeling that he had been venturing out into a new world, a world of beautiful sadness, of delicate shades of emotion that he didn't usually come into contact with. But the girl's giggle broke his rapture. The giggle was almost coarse, exciting on another scale, the excitement of a low bar with

33

a juke box going and beer slopped into cheap straight glasses.

"Yes. Mother had a lover but the affair broke up. He came for several years."

"His name, miss?"

"Vleuten, Jan Vleuten, but everybody calls him the baboon, the blond baboon."

"You liked him?" The question was irrelevant at that point and came up suddenly, but the giggle had shaken the commissaris too.

"Oh, yes."

"But the connection broke up, you said. When was that, miss?"

"About two years ago, I think. She would still see him occasionally but then it stopped altogether. He worked for the company, but when he left the affair ended too."

"I see. Well, I think we can go now. We have to see you a few more times, but that will be later. You need a good rest now. You're sure that your mother didn't have a visitor tonight, aren't you, miss? If we knew she had and we knew who the visitor was our work would be easier and take up less time."

"I don't know, there was only one glass on the table when I came down. I didn't hear the bell, but I may have been in the kitchen here when the bell rang. It isn't a very loud bell."

Cardozo jumped up again. "Shall I check the bell, sir?"

"No, that's all right. Thanks for the coffee, miss." The commissaris was attempting to get up and his face grimaced with pain. Cardozo helped him to his feet.

3

The commissaris wouldn't let Gabrielle accompany him to the front door but said good-bye at the door of her room. He held her shoulder lightly as he said his good-night, having nudged Cardozo into the direction of the staircase. There was a gentleness in his touch that seemed to reach her. She no longer purred; her voice had become slightly hoarse instead. She left the door open as she walked back into her room and he closed it, for he had heard the constables come in to fetch the corpse. They were maneuvering awkwardly, bumping the stretcher against a wall. A trickle of water ran from the sodden body and the head flopped. The victory that Grijpstra had seen in Elaine Carnet's face earlier in the night was still there, but the joyous expression wasn't very substantial as her head moved past the commissaris. A thin victory, reached through great agony, the agony of a useless life. The commissaris had only a glimpse of the victim, but the moment cut into his perception and the shock bared his long yellowish teeth and aggravated the cold pain in his legs so that he stumbled and had to support himself against a wall.

Death was his game, of course, and as the officer in charge of Amsterdam's murder brigade he dealt with it continuously, but he had never made his peace with death.

On a few occasions he had seen people die and seen fear change into surprise, a surprise mingled with horror. This was the first time he had seen surprise mingled with joy, or was joy the wrong definition?

The question stayed in his mind as the car made its way carefully through the southern part of the old city. Grijpstra and Cardozo were on the back seat, both sunk into apathy, and de Gier was steering, trying to see something through the waves of water that the nervous little wipers couldn't deal with. After a few minutes the rain suddenly stopped, and the commissaris saw the torn and broken trunk of a weeping willow that had graced a small square for as long as he could remember. Large puddles of inky water were almost brought to foam by a sweep of the gale. He still saw Elaine Carnet's head, the bedraggled clown's mask of a middle-aged woman. Who cares? he thought. The dead are dumped and we tear into the living flesh of the killer if we can find him and frazzle the nerves of a number of suspects in the process. His gloom, cold edged with razor-blade cuts of the pain in his legs, increased and he braced himself in defense. He had to find refuge in the calm that he knew to be in his mind as well. This was a murder case like any other and it would have to be approached by normal methods. He would go into the mess tomorrow, for a mess it was. He only hoped that it was a simple mess that could be cleared quickly. Like de Gier and Grijpstra, he felt sure that there had been a crime, although he wouldn't forget the easier explanation of a combination of accidental causes.

Gales are known to unsettle people's minds. Mrs. Carnet had probably been a nervous woman, lonely and fearful. Her favorite spot was the porch with the ugly chairs and the TV set and a gramophone and old records that reminded her of her glamorous past. She also drank. The doctor would be able to tell him how much she drank, once he had done his tests. She had been drinking that evening. She might have fallen down her garden stairs, why not? The broken wineglass in the garbage container, the cigar butts with plastic mouthpieces, the wedding ring on the floor

. . . clues that might lead to nothing.

But he didn't think so. The meeting with Gabrielle had only deepened his suspicions. De Gier was probably right, she had been acting too well. Grijpstra, as usual, wouldn't commit himself. Cardozo was too young and inexperienced, he would only say what he had heard, seen, smelled, felt, tasted, as a young detective should. But Cardozo's assistance would be important, for he had met Gabrielle before her mother died.

The commissaris was organizing his attack on the knot of lies, schemes, hidden emotions, suppressed fears, that had already shown itself in part, but he got caught up again in the gale and in what the gale was doing to the city that had been his hunting ground for over forty years. He knew Amsterdam as warm, friendly, comforting as a mother. He was used to riding through her streets, recognizing odd corners, feeling the spreading protection of old trees, the cool of waterways nibbling at quays built centuries ago out of cobblestones, each individually faced, each with its own growth of minute, fuzzy plants forming a green border to the small, blue-gray, lapping waves. Now the canals were hellish sewers, covered in yellow spray where they were lit up by swinging streetlights.

The sign of a drugstore came flying, and de Gier turned the wheel so that it sailed past and hit the street and broke, exploding into a cloud of plastic particles. He could hear Grijpstra grunt behind him. Two fire engines hurtled toward the Volkswagen and de Gier drove onto the sidewalk. The engine stalled, and they could hear the sirens of the red trucks, howling emptily.

"Must be on their way to a collapsed house."

The commissaris didn't acknowledge the sergeant's remark but struggled on with his thoughts.

They came to the avenue where the commissaris lived. The sergeant had guided the car onto the sidewalk again to avoid the fallen trees and to minimize the commissaris's exposure to the weather. When de Gier switched the engine off he looked at the commissaris's face and smiled. His chief seemed his usual calm self, slightly amused, neat, gentle. The discipline of a long life of continuous effort had reasserted itself, the commissaris's fear had been forced back into its lair, where it sat, cramped and uncomfortable, wrapped into itself, a black shapeless monstrosity, powerless and pathetic.

"I'll see you three gentlemen tomorrow at nine," the commissaris said cheerfully. "Don't think about the case tonight, we'll tackle it in the morning, it'll still be fresh."

"Sir," the three men said. The sergeant wanted to get out of the car to open the commissaris's door, but the little old man was in the street already, stumbling to the front door that was being held open by his wife, whose housecoat was being blown to the side. They saw her reach out and pull him in.

4

The large room on the third floor of Amsterdam police headquarters breathed a quiet atmosphere of comfortable respectability. The room had been neutral when the commissaris moved into it, many years back. The service had supplied him with furniture—a desk, some chairs, some tables—a carpet, all noncommittal, gray and brown, well made but without any appreciable style. The commissaris had left the furniture where it had been put down but had built his own feeling around them. There was a profusion of plants on the windowsills now, and on the walls hung magnificent seventeenth-century portraits wangled from the stores of the Rijksmuseum, showing bright-eyed gentlemen dressed in velvet, with hooked noses and flamboyant beards, men of past authority who had helped to form the city and contributed to its splendor of canals reflecting a few thousand ornamental but still simple gables. The faces on the portraits showed an unusual degree of intelligence and insight and a glint of humor, and it was difficult, at first glance, to relate the direct lineage that linked them to the commissaris, the mousy old man who now faced his three assistants. The commissaris's shape could sink away into any crowd, and it would be possible to pass him several times in an hour without retaining the slightest recollection. And yet, by studying his face and the way he carried his sparse frame, much could be seen. The three detectives were seeing more of it now They were also listening.

"A mess," the commissaris had said. "This case is a mess, and I wish we could leave it alone. We could, easily. The lady had a little too much to drink, she was upset because of the gale, she slipped, she fell, she broke her neck. A report, that's all we have to write. I could catch the whole event in half a page and everybody here would accept my version. What do you think?"

There were some mumbles that evolved into one audible word pronounced by Grijpstra: "No."

"No?"

"No, sir." Grijpstra's bulky body filled the commissaris's chair of honor, a heavy piece of furniture capped by wooden lions' heads snarling on each side of his wide shoulders. Grijpstra felt fine. He had got up early and had been able to shave and have breakfast in peace, and he had found a clean suit and his favorite shirt, light blue with a detachable white collar, bought at half-price at the last sale of Amsterdam's best clothing store.

"Why not?" the commissaris asked. "Do you think we have anything to go on? The clues point to a family fight culminating in manslaughter. We don't have to presuppose ill will or planning. I am reasonably sure that we'll come up with the reconstruction of a situation where tempers ran high because of irritation aggravated by the unusual weather. The lady was shoved and fell. There was no wish to kill. The case may fizzle out in court after a few hundred hours of work on our part, and we may have made some blunders on the way that may increase the suffering of some of our fellow beings we haven't even met so far. You think we should go ahead?"

"Yes, sir."

"De Gier?"

De Gier spread his long muscular hands. His large eyes gleamed; there seemed to be a slight movement in the up-swept ends of his mustache. "No, sir, you shouldn't ask me. If you start the investigation I will work on it, with pleasure, I may say. There's a puzzle. The girl was lying, I think, and I would like to know the significance of the clues, of the whole situation. But perhaps there is nothing there; the gale gave a strange impact last night, everything was different. But I have no opinion about whether or not to take the case. Maybe you are right, maybe we'll do more harm than good.''

"And maybe we shouldn't concern ourselves with that,'' Grijpstra said quietly. "We are the police, we are maintaining order, we have rules.''

"So if the rules lead to more disorder?'' the commissaris asked, but he didn't wait for Grijpstra's reply. "Never mind. We'll take the case. I am not asking you, Cardozo, I will ask you in a few years' time. That doesn't mean I don't value your opinion but it has to be formed first.'' He got up and walked over to the young detective, sitting straight up on a hard-backed chair. Cardozo got patted on his curly head and the commissaris retreated behind his glass-topped desk. "Right, so we proceed. This is the way I would want you to start out. We have the following persons involved: Elaine Carnet, dead, but she left her corpse that has to be investigated. I want to know whether the wedding ring fits easily on her finger. Cardozo, you can go to the morgue when this conference is over. Does anybody have the ring?''

Grijpstra pointed at a carton standing next to his chair. "In there, sir.''

"Good. I saw the fingerprint report. Surfaces have been wiped clean, in the expert's opinion anyway. The statement wouldn't hold in court—doorknobs are often in touch with garments and the result is a fingerprintless doorknob—but for us it is a clue. A suspect hiding tracks, or somebody else's tracks. There is more information that is of interest. The doctor claims that Elaine Carnet had been drinking to the point of intoxication and that she was a habitual drinker but not quite an alcoholic. His report is documented properly and it will hold in court. So Elaine was drunk last night; her lack of self-control may have made her say something that invited an attack and got her pushed down the stairs. Who pushed her? The mysterious cigar smoker? We have Gabrielle Carnet, Elaine's partner Mr. Bergen, and Elaine's former lover the blond baboon, a man called Jan Vleuten, and that's all so far, right?"

"Mr. de Bree, sir," Cardozo said. "The suspected dog poisoner, the man I interviewed or tried to interview but he slammed the door in my face."

"Good. We have him too, but he doesn't want to see us. We need more material against him, preferably statements by witnesses who saw him feeding the dog. Maybe the witnesses can be found; the garden in which the poisoning took place can be seen by a fairly large number of people, the inhabitants of the houses next and opposite the Carnet house, opposite the rear of the Carnet house, that is. Something for you, Cardozo. Once you have been to the morgue you can do your rounds. If you produce some evidence, no matter how vague, we have a stronger case against your nasty Mr. de Bree and we can haul him in for questioning. So far he is out of reach although I could try to bluff him."

"That leaves Gabrielle Carnet, Mr. Bergen, and this blond baboon, sir."

"Yes, sergeant. We don't know much about Gabrielle yet, in spite of my questioning last night. She'll have to be seen again, maybe also by Cardozo, for he has met her twice now and there should be some contact between them. I don't think you should go, de Gier. You said you didn't like her, is that right?"

De Gier nodded.

"Lack of sympathy doesn't make questioning any easier, so Grijpstra can go. You and I can see Mr. Bergen and this blond baboon. It can all be done today. We may come up with other suspects, I hope not, however. There shouldn't be too many suspects. Mrs. Carnet had a glass of wine with her killer and received him on the porch, not in her splendid living room. She knew the killer intimately and she gave me the impression of being a lonely woman, but the impression may be wrong. It *was* a strange night and the gale may have influenced our reasoning. Maybe Elaine Carnet had a lot of intimate friends and maybe all the friends hated her. Who knows, but we should find out today."

The room was silent. A constable brought coffee and Cardozo served.

"Any questions?"

"The safe, sir, and the portrait."

The commissaris rubbed his hands. "The safe and the portrait," he said slowly. "Yes. Um. Um, um, um, um. Very good of you, adjutant. You said that you and de Gier found a wall safe hidden by a painting while Cardozo and I were upstairs questioning Gabrielle. The safe contained a box, an old-fashioned cigar box, and the box had three hundred guilders* in it and some change. So perhaps it hadn't been opened, for the money was there. But according to the fingerprint expert the safe's handle had been wiped clean. You can ask Gabrielle about the safe when you see her today. Maybe she knows if her mother kept a lot of money in it. And then there was the painting hung over the safe. We don't have it here, do we?"

"No, sir."

"A portrait of Elaine Carnet done when she was young. She was standing next to a piano and she was singing."

"Yes, sir. The painting was signed 'Wertheym.' "

The commissaris half-closed his eyes and breathed out sharply. "Well, what would that mean? Just a portrait done by a painter. But we might visit the painter. There may have been some relationship between him and Elaine and he may be able to tell us about her. Very likely not, but we won't pass it up. Why don't you visit this painter, adjutant, while Cardozo sniffs around the area of the Carnet house, and then you two can meet later to see Gabrielle. Will that do?"

"Certainly, sir."

The commissaris looked at his watch. "Ten o'clock, we can finish our coffee in comfort and then all set out. Cardozo?"

Cardozo shot forward on his chair, almost toppling off.

* A guilder is $0.40, or £0.25.

His eagerness made de Gier smile and he pulled his mustache to mask his merriment.

"You are the only one who has something to work on. So far all our suspects are too smooth to grab. They have plenty of little hooks where we could fasten a string, but we don't know where to look for them. But you have your Mr. de Bree, and we can be almost sure that he did try to kill that dog. We could hold on to him if you can produce some evidence, the slightest evidence will do. He is our only clear contact with the Carnet household: he knows both Elaine and Gabrielle, his garden borders on theirs, neighbors always know quite a lot about each other. It would be too much to expect that you can find witnesses to the actual death of Elaine—it must have happened late at night, when the gale was having its climax and it was raining heavily. But try anyway, take your time, visit everybody who lives in a house with a view of the Carnet garden."

"Yes, sir."

Grijpstra's eyelids dropped as he looked away from Cardozo's bright face. The young detective reminded him of a fellow pupil at school, a wiry little get-ahead, an eager-beaver pup that would drool whenever he could catch a teacher's attention. The pupil always got straight A's. He was a general now, in charge of Dutch tank brigades, clumsily plowing down fences on German farms. Grijpstra was glad he wasn't a general, but then, perhaps generals can get divorces easily. He stopped the thought. Whatever he tried to think about these days would always lead to divorce.

The commissaris stubbed out his cigar and the detectives got up but sat down again. The cigar hadn't been the right signal. The commissaris had left his desk and was wandering about the room, studying his plants.

He mumbled to himself, took an atomizer from a shelf, and sprayed a large fern that hung from the ceiling on a chain.

"Lovely, look at this new sprout, it's all curled up like a bishop's stave." The detectives stood around the fern and made appropriate remarks. Only de Gier seemed really interested.

"You should have some ferns in your apartment, de Gier, they are both decorative and tranquilizing."

"My cat will jump them and tear their leaves, sir."

"Really? Tabriz? I thought she was a pleasant, sedate female. Well, just hang it high enough. It'll rest your mind as you lie on your bed and it will give you good ideas. The mind really only functions well when it's properly calmed." He walked back to his desk and sat down. His small dried-out, almost yellow hands rested on the tabletop. He didn't hear the detectives as they trooped out of the room.

"Sir?" de Gier asked from the door.

"Hmm? Yes. I'll meet you in the courtyard in fifteen minutes, sergeant. We'll visit Mr. Bergen first, the Carnet partner—find the address of Carnet and Company, please, they deal in furniture. I think I've seen their building, near the Pepperstraat somewhere."

The sergeant closed the door slowly. He heard the last two words the commissaris said. "Messy. Yagh!"

5

The building in the Pepperstraat consisted of six small, three-storied houses joined on the inside while still retaining their apparent individualities. Each house had its own ornamentation, very different from the others if observed carefully, but the overall effect created unity again. The commissaris stood in the narrow street while de Gier drove off again to find a parking place, and looked up to get a good view. He wondered why the sixteenth and seventeenth centuries had given rise to so much perfect beauty and how the beauty could have got lost for so long. It was coming back now, there was hope again, but it had been gone for hundreds of years, drab years that had built other parts of the city, long cramped streets of soot-soaked grayness lining up houses that were an insult to humanity with their cramped quarters and stark, forbidding rooflines.

A sign, hung from a cast-iron bar, read CARNET & CO., FURNITURE, IMPORT & WHOLESALE in small neat lettering. Through several open windows on the first floor the clatter of electric typewriters could be heard. An elderly couple, probably a storekeeper and his wife, were received at the narrow green front door of the first gable by a smooth-looking young man in a tailored suit. A salesman welcoming customers. Elaine Carnet had obviously built up a good business. He felt sorry now that he hadn't taken time to study the corpse's face more carefully. From the glimpse he remembered he could detect neither efficiency nor the polite ruthlessness that marks a success in business.

He grinned, maybe he was too hard on the trade. But he had always felt the cutting power of the traders' brains whenever he had dealt with them. There might be more friendliness, more understanding, in the smaller merchants, the dealers who were in direct contact with consumers. When business works on wholesale and factory levels facial expressions change. He would have to base himself on what he had seen during that brief moment when the constables carried Mrs. Carnet's body out to the hearse. He had only seen an elderly woman, lonely, defeated, unconcerned about such matters as turnover and profit margin and cost control. The business would have been built up by others, although she might have owned the lion's share of the company's stock. But he had also seen that extraordinary expression of ghoulish delight.

De Gier came running around the corner. "Sorry, sir, I parked her at some distance."

"It's a pity my legs always trouble me, otherwise I could use a bicycle again. To try and use a car these days is more fuss than pleasure. Let's go in, sergeant."

Bergen came to the door. He had been advised to expect a visit from the police by the commissaris's secretary. The man fitted in with the image the firm presented. Not a young man, somewhere between fifty and sixty—the energetic way in which he carried himself might blur a few years. Short silvery gray hair, brushed till it shone, heavy jowls, close shaven, eyes that shone with nervous energy behind heavy lenses framed in gold. An impeccably dressed man, there was no fantasy in the clothes. A dark blue suit, a white shirt, a tie of exactly the same shade as the suit. The sort of man who is chosen by TV commercials to tell the ladies about a new washing machine or some other expensive item that requires some faith before it can be purchased. Mr. Bergen's voice confirmed the impression he was making, a warm deep sound coming from a wide chest.

"Commissaris, sergeant, please follow me. My office is on the top floor, I'll show the way if you'll excuse my going ahead." He must have said it a thousand times, to customers, to suppliers, to tax inspectors.

De Gier was the last to climb the stairs and the commissaris was some six steps ahead of him. As he watched the commissaris's narrow back he hummed, "Creepy creepy little mouse, Trips into Mr. Bergen's house."

Bergen didn't know what he was up against. De Gier thought of the chief inspector who had been in charge of several murder cases some years before. He had liked to use an innocent, almost stupid approach to lure suspects into talking freely, but he had a sadistic side to his character. He always seemed to take pride in demolishing the suspects' defenses and to show them up, finally, for what they were, and the suspects, being human, invariably showed themselves to be little more than brown paper bags filled with farts, a term the chief inspector liked to use. It had never seemed to occur to him that he himself might also fit that definition, and that he might burst or tear if enough pressure were brought to bear on his flimsy outer shell. The commissaris, although he played the game along the same general lines as his colleague, never enjoyed his kills. De Gier wondered if Bergen were a legal prey. So far they had no reason to expect more than some information.

They were ushered into a vast room, half showroom, half office. There was a profusion of leather furniture, couches and easy chairs, and the commissaris and the sergeant were directed to a low settee apparently made of some very excellent cowhide, a choice piece that was no doubt worth a fortune, a perfect example of contemporary Italian design.

"Gentlemen," Bergen said slowly, keeping his voice on a low pitch that was clearly audible, "some coffee perhaps? A cigar?"

The coffee was served by Gabrielle, dressed in a khaki jumpsuit.

The policemen stood up to shake her hand and Gabrielle smiled and purred. They were asked to be seated again and she bent down to give them their cups. Her breasts were almost entirely visible in the low top of her suit. De Gier was interested, but only mildly. He couldn't understand the girl's preference for trousers, the outfit accentuated her rather short bent legs, the way her jeans had the night before. He noted a glint near her neck and concentrated to see what it was. Gabrielle saw his interest and paused longer than necessary. A plastic thread, de Gier thought, very thin, and some object at the end of it, small and brown and shiny, partly hidden by the breasts, stuck in between. A button, perhaps. Why would she wear a wooden button between her breasts? The thought didn't go deep and hardly registered.

"You work here too, Miss Carnet?"

"Only sometimes, when Mr. Bergen expects important customers in the showroom or when the firm is very busy. We're having a visitor this afternoon who buys for a chain of department stores, and Mr. Pullini is in town, of course."

The commissaris came to life. "Pullini? That's an Italian name, isn't it? Didn't you tell me yesterday that your mother started the business with furniture imported from Italy?"

Bergen had sat down near them, balancing his coffee cup gracefully. "That's right, commissaris. Most of our merchandise still comes from Italy, but in this room we only show the expensive items. We also sell a lot of mass-produced furniture and we have been specializing lately in chairs and tables that can be stacked. We started selling to restaurants and hotels and canteens and so forth, and last year we began doing business with the armed forces."

"You must be doing well, yet we are having a depression, are we not?"

Bergen smiled widely. "That's what the merchants say who fail, they'll always have a depression. I don't think there is any real trouble, apart from the high taxes, of course, that's one factor that may squeeze us all out of existence."

"How much are you selling?" the commissaris asked.

"Just a rough idea, you don't have to tell me if you don't want to. I'm being curious, that's all."

"Eight million last year." Bergen beamed. His polite awareness was clearly weakening, the policeman had made a good impression. "But that was a particularly good year, and a lot of that was army and navy business. Even so, we should do well again this year, even without any big contracts. The business is steady, fortunately. There will always be a good demand for furniture and we are well placed in the market."

The commissaris was nodding, a proud father admiring the antics of a child. The conversation flowed along until Bergen interrupted himself. "Mrs. Carnet," he said sadly, "my long-time partner, you are here to investigate her death, I presume?"

"Indeed."

"Do you suspect foul play, commissaris?"

The commissaris's head bent and the gesture reminded de Gier of his cat, Tabriz. Tabriz would drop her head to the side if she wasn't quite sure if she liked what he had heaped on her dish. "Perhaps not. There are some indications we can't explain at this point but they may fall into place and the death may very well be due to an accident. If that is so we would like to come to that conclusion with a minimal delay so that the case can be closed. What can you tell us about Mrs. Carnet, Mr. Bergen? Did she have any close friends, and did any of them visit her, perhaps last night, or did anybody at all visit her last night?"

Bergen's tight mouth curved downward. He appeared to be thinking hard. "No. I don't know what she did last night. I was home, working on a tree in my garden that was bumping against the roof. Elaine didn't come to the office yesterday, but then she hardly ever does these days. She is really semiretired and leaves the running of the business to me. We used to have a lot of contact in the old days, when we were making the firm grow, but that's all over now and has been for several years."

"Mother didn't have much of a routine," Gabrielle said. "She liked to get up late and then she would have breakfast in a restaurant somewhere and do some shopping and go to the hairdresser and she sometimes went to the movies. She only had her evening meal at home."

"I see." The commissaris got up, looked about, and sat down again.

"More coffee?" Gabrielle asked.

"No, erhm, no. I wonder if you would mind very much, Miss Carnet, if I asked you to let us talk to Mr. Bergen alone for a little while. I would like to ask some questions that, well, may embarrass you."

Gabrielle laughed and got up, taking the empty cups from the table. "Of course, but I don't get embarrassed easily. I am a modern girl, you know."

"Yes, yes," the commissaris said, still ill at ease. De Gier's eyes narrowed. He had seen it all before. The situation was shaping up nicely, manipulated detail by detail.

"Now," the commissaris said when Gabrielle had left the room, "I am sure you know why I asked Miss Carnet to leave us alone for a minute. If Mrs. Carnet was killed last night and didn't just slip and fall down her stairs—she had drunk a fair amount of wine, you know, Beaujolais, a strong wine, we found an empty bottle—she may have been killed by someone she was on intimate terms with. Would you know of such a person, sir?"

Bergen was thinking again. Evidently he wanted to be helpful but he was weighing his words. "Yes. I see what you mean. Well, Elaine did have a lover for several years, an employee of this firm, a man called Vleuten. He left us two years ago, rather suddenly."

"Because of any unpleasantness?"

"Yes." Bergen was scraping his throat industriously. "Yes, you might call it that. A nasty business. You see, Elaine fell in love with the baboon—that's his nickname, he rather looks like an ape, he didn't mind being called baboon. Elaine really fell for him, and he does have a nice personality, I'll say that for him. That was some time ago. Elaine was still in her forties then and rather attractive, she went to pieces later. The wine helped, but that's another matter."

"Related perhaps?" the commissaris suggested.

"Yes, related possibly. But there were other reasons, I think. The firm has grown so much that its mechanics became impossible for her to grasp. She could never understand the computerized bookkeeping and store records for instance; she liked to keep the records herself according to some old-fashioned system that she had mastered. She was hurt, I think, when we modernized our administration and most of her work became superfluous, and she began to withdraw. Her desk is over there. There's nothing on it anymore, not even a telephone. She doesn't really like to come in now. She doesn't know what is happening and she doesn't like to try and deal with anything anymore for fear that it may explode in her face."

"Yes." The commissaris's voice sounded thoughtful. "Yes, quite. A lost lonely woman, that's the impression I got from seeing her corpse."

The word "corpse" made Bergen wince and his hand moved quickly over his left cheek. He had made the gesture before, and de Gier noticed the nervous clasping of the hand after the movement was completed. He looked closely at Bergen's face. The left side seemed affected in some way, the eye looked larger than the right and the corner of the mouth drooped a little. Perhaps the man had survived a stroke. When Bergen spoke again some letters appeared slightly transformed. The *p*'s and *b*'s popped. De Gier shrugged. He was collecting some very useful information, so Bergen had suffered a stroke once, so what.

"An affair with an employee, that must have been unpleasant for you. What was Mr. Vleuten's position in the firm? Was he a salesman?"

"Sales director. He did very well for us. Some of our largest accounts are his work. The baboon was never an administrator and I don't think he could have run Carnet and Company, but he was certainly doing spectacular work in his own field."

The commissaris was lighting a small cigar. His voice had crossed the border between being conversational and amiable; the tension that de Gier had originally felt in Bergen's reactions was easing off.

"Yes, sales," the commissaris said, waving his cigar. "A business can do nothing without them, but good sales can be spoiled by bad administration. Did Mr. Vleuten aspire to become the head of this firm, was he a rival to you in any way?"

"No. The baboon didn't aspire to be anything other than what he was but he was a rival nevertheless, a most powerful rival, because Elaine was pushing the baboon right into my chair. And there wasn't just the business aspect to deal with. The baboon was Elaine's lover and she was cuddling him right here in this office, holding his hands, nibbling his ears, gazing into his eyes. You used the word 'embarrassing' just now, that's what it was, embarrassing. I felt a complete fool in my own office the minute the two came in. The baboon was always polite and charming, of course, but Elaine's behavior made me sick to my stomach. If I brought in some business, and I do that all the time, of course, the matter was completely ignored even if it was a contract involving a million guilders, but if the baboon sold a kitchen table and four matching chairs to a dear old lady running a store in the country we all had to sing the national anthem."

The policemen laughed and Bergen laughed with them, pleased with his little joke.

"So?"

"So I had to drive the matter to its peak. I simply couldn't stand it any longer. We had a meeting, the three of us, and I offered to resign and sell them my shares. It was a big risk, for I could have lost out easily, but I was still gambling on Elaine's insight. She must have known that my experience was important to the company's future and that the baboon had only proved himself as a salesman, never as an administrator. But she didn't blink an eye."

"Really? But the baboon left and you still are here."

Bergen's right hand played with the hem of his jacket.

"Yes. He surprised me. He got up and walked over to that typewriter over there and wrote his letter of resignation. It was very decent of him. He had the whole company in the palm of his hand for a minute but he blew it away. Even if he couldn't have administered the business he could have found somebody else to do that part of the work. We were doing very well. He was, in fact, refusing a fortune.''

"And he left with nothing?"

"Just a few months' wages. Elaine offered him a year's income but he refused. I offered to accept his resignation in such a way that he would have qualified for unemployment benefits but he refused that too. He just shook my hand, kissed Elaine's cheek, and left. I haven't seen him since.''

"Not even in the street?"

"No.''

"And Mrs. Carnet? Did he break with her too then?"

"Yes, but she tried to make contact again. I heard her phone him. He's a good carpenter and she wanted him to fix something in her house. He may have come and the relationship may have continued in some way but I don't know, I always preferred not to ask.''

The commissaris got up and walked over to a window. "Not the sort of man who would have pushed her down the garden stairs.''

"No. The baboon isn't a violent man.''

"Are *you*, sir?'' The commissaris had turned to ask the question. It was asked in the same level tone he had used before but his eyes were fixed on Bergen's face.

"Violent?''

"Yes. Are you a violent man?''

Bergen's voice faltered. His left cheek seemed to sag more than before. The underlip had suddenly become slack and he was making an effort to answer the question. "No, no. I don't think so. I got into some fights at school and I had a scrap or two when I was in the army but that's gone now, I think it's not in me anymore.''

"We'll have to ask you whether you can prove where you were last night, Mr. Bergen. I realize these are unpleasant questions but we have to ask them.''

"I was at home, it wasn't the sort of night to go out.''

"Were you alone?''

"Yes, my wife is staying with relatives, she is having a little holiday in the country. My children are married already. I was alone."

"No visitors? Nobody telephoned you?"

"No."

"Well, that was only for the record." The commissaris was going to elaborate on his statement, but the telephone rang and Bergen walked to his desk to answer it.

"Mr. Pullini? Has he come already? Ask Miss Gabrielle to talk to him for a little while, I'm busy now. And don't send any calls through; if you take the numbers I'll phone them back." He put the phone down with some unnecessary force and turned to face his visitors again. "Pullini," he said slowly. "It's a day of problems."

De Gier's eyes hadn't left Bergen's face for the last few minutes. He was studying the deterioration of the left side of the man's head with fascination. The muscles of his cheek and mouth were slackening rapidly and he didn't think that Bergen had modified what was happening to his face. The sergeant thought of drawing the commissaris's attention to the phenomenon in some way when Bergen began to speak again.

"Pullini. If only the man himself had come again, but he sent his darling son."

"You're having trouble with your supplier? Pullini is still your main supplier, isn't that right?"

"Yes, we buy more than half our stocks from him. A good factory, steady and quick deliveries, excellent quality, but his prices are too high these days. That's why young Pullini is here, he has been here for two weeks already. I have found another factory in Milan that can supply us and they are more competitive than the Pullini concern. They also give a little more credit—credit is important to us, we have to hold large inventories."

"And Pullini doesn't want to come down in price?"

"Not so far."

"So why doesn't young Pullini leave? Or is he liking Amsterdam?"

Bergen grinned. The grin was definitely lopsided and de

Gier wondered if the commissaris was aware of their suspect's transformation. "Yes, he likes the high life here. Italians are still old-fashioned. The boy is having a good time, but he is hanging on for another reason. Old Pullini is also retired, like Elaine, and his concern is run by Francesco now, and Francesco has done a little underhanded maneuvering, or so I think, I can't prove it."

"Stealing from his father's business?"

"Perhaps. Papa Pullini is a tough old bird. He keeps his son on a short leash and Francesco has expensive ways, a brand-new Porsche, the best hotels, a little gambling—you know how it goes. Since Francesco took over we are given two invoices for every purchase. An official ninety percent invoice and an under-the-table ten percent invoice. I don't mind. On the ten percent invoices we have more credit; we keep them in a stack and pay them at the end of the year, in cash."

"And the ten percent goes into Francesco's pocket. I see. That's probably why he can't lower his prices, he's taking ten percent off already."

Bergen was nodding rapidly. He was evidently pleased that the commissaris saw the point so quickly.

"But," the commissaris said and raised a finger, "you say that you pay at the end of the year and we are in June now."

"I didn't make last year's payment. The money is still here, safely in the bank. I have been complaining about the Pullini price list and I have ignored Francesco when he kept on asking for his ten percent. I'm doing a little blackmailing, I suppose. It isn't nice of me, but we aren't always nice in business. I could switch over to the other company in Milan but I don't really want to do that either. The other company is too big, they might want to start up their own office here sometime and cut me out."

"Difficult," the commissaris agreed.

The interview was over, and the commissaris was near the door when he turned around. "Mrs. Carnet had a safe, Mr. Bergen, a small wall safe. We opened it with a key we found in her bag. There was a small amount in it, some three hundred guilders. You wouldn't know if she kept large amounts in that safe, would you?''

Bergen was holding his cheek and massaging it. ''No.'' he said after a while. ''I know she had a safe and there may have been a lot of money in it from time to time, she did have large amounts of cash sometimes, but I wouldn't know if there was any appreciable quantity in there last night. It's not the sort of thing she would talk to me about. Our conversations of the past few years were mostly about what movies to see, we both like the same sort of films.''

''You never had much social contact with Mrs. Carnet, had you?''

''Not really. I am married, my wife has always been rather jealous of Elaine, and later there was the baboon, of course.''

''Thank you, Mr. Bergen, you've been most helpful.''

''Did you notice his face, sir?'' de Gier asked as they walked back to the car.

The commissaris was looking at a garbage boat that was making a sharp corner in the canal. A young man, a boy almost, was turning its large wheel effortlessly and the heavy diesel engine controlling the barge's screw was churning up a perfect arc of thick frothy waves. Workmen were sawing a broken tree on the other side of the canal, with the boat pulling cables so that the thick elm wouldn't fall the wrong way.

''Two million trees down in the country, according to the radio,'' the commissaris said. ''Two million, I wonder how they can guess the number. The whole country is a mess and we have our own to play with. Yes, I noted Bergen's facial paralysis, sergeant. It must have started before we came, but he was going through a crisis while we talked to him.''

''A stroke, sir?''

''No, I don't think so, but I am sure he's telephoning his doctor right now. I thought I would have to cut my questioning off, but I had gone too far already.''

''But if he got upset to such an extent . . . .'' De Gier had stopped, but the commissaris kept on walking, and the sergeant had to sprint to catch up with him again.

"He must be guilty?"

"He might be."

"He might be, sure. And he might not be. We don't know how involved he was with the lady. And he may have other worries. That Pullini business may be much worse than he made it appear. I would like to see young Pullini. Try and find out where he's staying after you've dropped me off. Don't ask Mr. Bergen or Gabrielle. Find him through the hotel records. It shouldn't be difficult to run him down. If he doesn't expect us to look for him and if we suddenly show up the questioning may be more, what's the word, 'deadly'."

De Gier steered the commissaris's black Citroën through the narrow alleys near the center of the old city. They got stuck a few times and had to wait for trucks and motorized tricycles unloading, and every now and then they would run into a detour caused by municipal workmen clearing fallen trees. Most of the glass of broken windows had already been swept up. The city still looked desolate, however, and the commissaris's mood fitted in with the general devastation.

"Bah," he said as the car turned into its reserved space on the courtyard of police headquarters. "We'll have to push ourselves, sergeant. I want this case to be over in a few days, in a week at the most. There's still some time before lunch to find Francesco Pullini. I hope Grijpstra and Cardozo will be back soon with something tangible. With four men on the job we should be able to cut through their nonsense quickly. There are other projects I'd like to be working on."

De Gier had switched the Citroën's engine off and was waiting for the car to give its customary sigh before starting to sink down to its lowest point. The vehicle's fluid suspension system always gave him a sensuous sensation, he was grinning in the split second of anticipation.

"You noticed that Mr. Bergen didn't smoke?"

"Yes, sir. He didn't smoke while we were with him but I saw a nicotine stain on his index finger. He smokes cig-

arettes, I saw a packet of Gauloises on his desk. He's probably trying to give it up."

"Giving it up," the commissaris repeated slowly. "I
have been watching the inspector lately. He is also trying
to give up smoking but he isn't making much headway. He
told me that he is now smoking a brand he doesn't like.
Maybe Mr. Bergen doesn't like cigars with plastic mouthpieces, or would that be too far-fetched, sergeant?"

The Citroën had finished its sigh and the sergeant was
alert again. He hadn't understood everything the commissaris said, but the sound of his superior's words was still
in his ears and he could reconstruct the question.

"He could have been at the Carnet house last night, sir,
and he might have a reason for wanting to have Mrs. Carnet
out of the way. Maybe she doesn't come to the company
often, but she does control it, legally anyway—she had
three-quarters of the shares."

"So we'll have to find out if there was any tension between them, some recent disagreement, something to do
with the company's policy perhaps. Yes." The commissaris
had been talking briskly and he opened the door and almost
jumped out, but he had to hold on to the car as a fresh flow
of pain burned through his legs.

"I'll find this Pullini man and the baboon, Mr. Vleuten,
sir. I'll phone you as soon as I know their addresses."

The commissaris was limping ahead as the building's
alarm system came on. Short hysterical bursts of a two-
toned horn split the quiet of the yard and a glass door burst
open, pushed by a young man in torn jeans and a dirty
jacket. He was running toward the gate, where two uniformed constables had lowered the beam and were protecting it, their guns out.

De Gier was running too. He cut the young man off and
dived for his legs, bringing him down with such force that
the dust of the yard came up in a small cloud. The commissaris had frozen in his tracks and watched the commo-
tion. The constables pulled the prisoner to his feet and
handcuffed him. De Gier was sadly inspecting a tear in his
jacket. Plainclothes detectives and more constables sur-

rounded the prisoner and half marched, half carried him back to the building. The commissaris stopped a detective.

"What are the charges against your man?"

"Robbery, sir, attempted manslaughter, drug dealing. We may come up with a pimping charge too, a girl brought in a complaint this morning."

"Bad case eh?"

"Yes, sir, a hopeless case. It might have been better if he had got himself shot, he'll spend the rest of his life in jail or the nuthouse. The psychiatrists have been looking at him but they don't seem to be able to classify the trouble. As far as we're concerned he's dangerous. He keeps on attacking the guards, he bit the chief guard just now."

The detective ran after his colleagues; the commissaris turned around. De Gier was still looking at his jacket.

"Are you all right, sergeant?"

"Yes, sir. I'll have to get another jacket, I'll do it now. I have a suit at the dry-cleaning place around the corner. This jacket has had it, I think. Even if I have it repaired the tear will still show."

"The police will pay. I am going to my office, de Gier."

The commissaris's mood didn't improve until he was back behind his desk and looking at his fern, which was catching the sun and showing its leaves in an almost unnatural glitter of sparkling green.

"Very nice," the commissaris said. "But you are one aspect of nature. I am dealing with another, and it's rotten, brown, dog-eared, moldy, smelly with disease."

He made the moves that had never failed to restore his equanimity. He lit a small cigar, telephoned for coffee, and began to walk around his office. He fed his plants after having mixed the right quantity of fertilizer into a plastic watering can. He sprayed the fern with slow bursts of a small glass atomizer. His telephone rang.

"I have the hotel, sir, the Pulitzer. Francesco Pullini is in his room now, according to the desk clerk. I also have the baboon's address, he lives on the Amsteldijk. According to the number he lives on the best part of the dike, where it overlooks the river close to the Thin Bridge."

"You haven't spoken to either of the suspects?"

"No, sir."

"We'll go and surprise them. I'll meet you in the courtyard in a minute. We might tackle young Pullini first."

The commissaris finished his coffee and rested his eyes on the fern again, the central ornament of the bright room.

The sergeant was waiting for him in the Citroën and got out when he saw his chief cross the yard.

"How did the gale treat your balcony last night, de Gier?"

The sergeant smiled ruefully. "Badly, sir. I've lost almost everything. The lobelia bush survived, but it sat on the floor in a concrete box Public Works let me have some time ago. The rest have gone. The geraniums and the begonias are torn to shreds. Some of them were blown away, pots and all, and the window of my bedroom is cracked."

"So?" There was some poignancy to the single word, and the sergeant's expressive eyes stared gently at the commissaris.

"I've ordered new plants, sir, but the greenhouse won't deliver them. The garage sergeant said he could let me have one of his pickups for a few hours, maybe I'll get the plants later in the day. I also ordered a new window but it may take weeks to arrive, the glass merchants are having the time of their lives right now. What about your house, sir?"

"Some damage. My wife is taking care of it."

"And the turtle, sir?"

The commissaris grinned. "The turtle is fine. I saw him trying to plow through the rubbish in the garden this morning. The ground is covered with broken branches and glass and the garden chairs of the neighbors, but the turtle just plows on. He looked quite cheerful, I thought."

"Maybe he'll be reincarnated as a police detective."

The commissaris touched de Gier's sleeve. "He has the right character. Let's go, sergeant."

"Yes, sir." The Citroën moved to the gate, where the constables were raising the barrier. De Gier braked to give way to a police truck loaded with a platoon of constables dressed in riot uniforms and armed with carbines. The truck had all its lights on and was sounding its siren.

"What's up?" he asked the constables at the barrier.

"Turks, they are having a gunfight somewhere, or Moroccans, I forget now, I heard it on the intercom just now. This is the second truck already. A big fight, automatics and everything."

De Gier sighed. He thought of Gabrielle's bowed legs. There wouldn't be a gunfight in this case. But as he followed in the wake of the screaming riot truck his feeling changed. Something might happen to make the case worthwhile, something usually happened. He looked at the small neat body of the commissaris and had to restrain himself not to pat the old man's shoulder affectionately.

6

Cardozo sipped his tea and smiled politely. He had been listening to the old lady for quite a while now. She was telling him about her recent hospitalization. The old lady's sister was waiting for a chance to say something too. A related subject, no doubt, something to do with varicose veins or the cartilage between the spine's vertebrae that wears away in old age and causes pains. Cardozo put his cup down and picked up a cookie and nibbled on it.

"Yes." he said. He arranged a proper expression of commiseration. It sat on his face like a thin plastic mask. Underneath there was nothing but raw impatience, but the mask fitted well. The ladies' birdlike voices prattled on. He had to go through all of it. He even knew their ages now. Seventy-eight, eighty-two. That's old. They wouldn't live much longer, but they were alive now and they had seen something and their statements would be acceptable to a judge, and Constable First Class Cardozo meant to get those statements.

He felt his pocket. The pen was there, so was his notebook. He would write out two statements and have them signed individually—the judge wouldn't like a joint statement. Whatever the two ladies had seen they had seen on their own, and the judge would want to know what they had seen in their own words. They had said they had seen something. They had seen Mr. de Bree, that nasty, ill-mannered man with the fat-face. Men shouldn't have fat faces, didn't the detective think so? Sure, he thought so. As nasty as his cat. Mr. de Bree's cat also had a fat face. And he was always catching the nice little birds; he had even caught the thrush that sang so beautifully, and chomped on the poor little thing and spread its feathers all over Mr. de Bree's garden. The old ladies had watched the onslaught through their binoculars. Weren't they nice binoculars? Alice had specially fetched them to show them to the detective. Beautiful copper binoculars, they don't make them like that anymore these days. She and her sister used to take them to the theater and to the opera. But that was a long time ago.

"Yes," Cardozo said. He wasn't going to ask more questions. He had asked them already, they knew exactly what he wanted, and they would tell him, in their own time. He glanced at his watch. Twenty minutes gone, and another two hours on the rest of his search. He had been everywhere, in any house that had a view of the Carnet garden. Nobody had seen anything, but everybody knew Mr. de Bree. A nasty man, he knew that by now, he knew it by his own experience. He hadn't forgotten the red scowling face glaring at him before the door banged with such force that a particle of plaster from the porch's ceiling had dropped at his feet.

He had been given several descriptions of the de Bree cat, a pampered monstrosity with a half-orange, half-black face, which gave the beast two appearances, depending on which side he was approached, but they were both bad. The cat was the terror of the gardens and the main source of the torn ears and bad wounds of other cats. He had also heard reports on Paul, the Carnet dog. Paul was nice. An intelligent, jolly dog who had successfully defended his domain against the de Bree cat, until he was poisoned.

"There he is," the old lady called Alice said and tugged at Cardozo's sleeve. He saw the cat, jumping leisurely across the liguster hedge dividing the de Bree and Carnet properties. "Big, isn't he? Twenty pounds of bad cat."

And then they told him, whispering, hissing, glancing over their shoulders to see if some mysterious shadow in the room were listening in. They had seen de Bree feeding Paul. Chopped steak, they were sure of it. They had trained their binoculars on him, they had seen every detail of the murderous attempt. Two days ago now, in the afternoon. The Carnet ladies weren't in and Paul was playing by himself in the garden, snapping at flies and dancing about, throwing his little pink rubber ball. And de Bree had come out with the meat and Paul had eaten it.

"But why didn't you tell the Carnet ladies?" Cardozo asked pleasantly, holding a respectful expression that belied the accusation in his question. He was the favorite nephew visiting his two old aunties and he wanted to know why they did things.

"Oh, but that would have been terrible. We *did* think about it but we didn't, you see, because they would have been so unhappy."

"Really?"

"Really."

"But you could have told us, the police."

Yes, they could have, but they didn't have a telephone and it was such a long walk to the nearest station and they weren't so young anymore.

"I am seventy-eight," Alice said.

"And I am eighty-two," Alice's sister said.

Cardozo brought out his notebook and prepared two statements. They didn't want to sign them. They didn't want any trouble.

"But Paul is still alive, he'll be playing in the garden soon. You don't want Mr. de Bree to poison him again, do you?"

"No."

But they still didn't want to sign the statement. Mr. de Bree wouldn't like it. He had bumped Alice's leg once with his car and he hadn't even got out to help her up. He was a *nasty* man, maybe next time he wouldn't just bump Alice, maybe the next time he would *kill* her.

"Never," Cardozo said. "Not with us around. We are the police, you see, we protect you, but we can only protect you if you help us." He waved the ball-point encouragingly. "Just a little signature, right here."

Alice signed, and then the sister signed too. They didn't want to read the statements, they didn't have their spectacles on.

"Where *are* my spectacles, Alice?" the sister asked. "You always mislay them."

"*What?*" Alice asked in a suddenly shrill voice.

"Thank you very much, ladies, thank you *very* much."

The argument went on as he ran down the stairs. He had come up with something, something positive, concrete, undeniable. He whistled as he banged the front door, and turned the corner. He waved at the de Bree door as he ran past it.

He remembered that there was a telephone booth at the end of the street. Grijpstra wasn't in but he was put through to the commissaris's secretary. "You are not to go and see Miss Carnet just now but to report to the commissaris later. He has gone away with the sergeant and the adjutant isn't back yet."

"So what am I to do?" Cardozo's voice shot up in indignation.

"Well, I don't know," the secretary's voice said coolly. "Surely you can find some work? The detectives' city patrols are always short of men, Sergeant Sietsema was asking for you. He's on duty this afternoon and he needs company."

"Oh, very well, I'll be back as soon as I can."

"Good boy." She hung up.

"Aren't I?" Cardozo asked the street. The telephone booth's door slammed behind him. "Aren't I? I got what they wanted me to get and I want to tell them about it and they aren't there. They're drinking coffee and smoking cigars and passing the time of day." He glared at the peaceful street.

But Amsterdam is a helpful city, it provides comfort in subtle ways. A woman came past, pushing a perambulator containing identical twins facing each other solemnly from their pink wraps, vaguely resembling Grijpstra in his better moments. An old man with long hair strode on the opposite pavement whistling a Bach cantata. A girl on a red bicycle came around the corner. She wore a sleeveless blouse, unbuttoned, and nothing underneath. A well-shaped girl. Cardozo winked at the girl and she winked back and he began to walk to his car. Not such a bad day after all.

But he felt a little uptight again when he started the Volkswagen. A constable at the next intersection raised his hand. The Volkswagen drove on slowly. The constable whipped out a whistle and blew it. Cardozo's foot stayed on the accelerator. He crossed the intersection and stopped, watching the constable in his rearview mirror. The constable was running.

"Didn't you see me?"

"Sure. I don't know what's the matter with me. I saw you, I saw you giving the stop sign, but I kept on driving. I must be going crazy."

The constable bent down and peered into Cardozo's face. "It sometimes happens," he whispered confidentially. "I see it every now and then. I've thought of several explanations. Some subconscious protest, perhaps, or a hidden aggression, something like that. Have you done this before?"

"No."

"First time, eh? Well, maybe it means nothing. Maybe you're just tired. But if it happens again you might see a psychiatrist. What do you do for a living?"

"I'm a police detective."

The constable's eyebrows shot up and he stepped back to study the car. He jumped forward and pushed his head into the window. Cardozo pointed at the police radio under the dashboard and fished out his plastic identification.

"Get away," the constable said.

"But . . ."

"Come on, get off. *Off!*" The constable walked back to the intersection. He was looking at the pavement and dragging his feet.

7

WERTHEYM, the plate on the door read, PORTRAIT
PAINTER.

There was nothing particular about the door and there
was nothing to prevent Adjutant Grijpstra from pressing the
bell but he didn't. He stood with his hands folded and
waited. He had been enjoying himself so far and he didn't
want to interrupt the steady flow of well-being that had
begun to soak into him from the moment he had left his
little house that morning. There was a small black cloud at
the end of the flow and he meant to keep it away for as
long as he could, a process that would be possible if he
consciously experienced the small moments that his working day would present. The black cloud was his return
home. He definitely didn't want to go home.

His wife, the blob of semi-solid fats, dirty and bad-tem-
pered, that had grown slowly out of the girl he had once
married, was gradually filling the two floors of their home,
pushing him to the wall, seeping into his peace, the peace
he built up during the day. One day he wouldn't go home
anymore. He didn't want to see her leaning on the kitchen
table that squeaked under her weight, leaning on the creak-
ing railing on the stair landing, leaning on the cracked windowsill. It was hard for her to stand now. It was also hard
for her to sit down, for the effort of getting up again might

break the few chairs that were still in one piece.

But, where could he go if he didn't go home? He was spending afterhours' time in his room at headquarters, he was eating out as much as he could, but he still had to go home to sleep. He cursed slowly, articulating the syllables. But then he promised himself he wouldn't think of the little black cloud; it would come on its own, without him thinking about it. His hand reached out slowly and pressed the bell.

The door opened at once.

"Mr. Wertheym?"

"Yes, I don't . . ."

"I am a police detective, sir, here is my card. Just a few questions, may I come in?"

"Certainly, certainly, I thought you wanted your portrait painted. I don't do men, you see, only women. I was going to tell you that, saves a lot of chatter. Come in."

The man could only be a painter. His appearance was a perfect combination of the number of attributes that make up the idea "painter" in the average perceptive mind. A small goatee, high forehead, bright eyes, a beret on the gray locks, an apron smeared with assorted colors—Wertheym was undoubtedly an artist. But there was nothing artistic about his house. The furniture had been taken straight from the showroom of a lower-middle-class store. The imitation fireplace with its licking gas flames creeping over iron birch logs complete with bark was in the worst possible taste. A calendar showing a plump girl in a glued-on flowery miniskirt that could be lifted up hung next to a triangular arrangement of plastic and tin replicas of Spanish swords. Different types of paper flowers had been matched into a bouquet that had lost both color and resilience.

Grijpstra's lips parted in a thin snarl. He also mumbled, "Home sweet home."

"Pardon?"

"I was just thinking that my wife would like this room."

"Would she now?" Wertheym offered a chair, one of a set of four, chrome framed and upholstered with strips of shiny green vinyl. "Not too hot for you here? This house is on the cold side of the street, never gets any sun. I keep the fire going but people say it's stuffy in here, don't notice it myself."

"Quite all right, thank you."

Grijpstra didn't open the conversation. He almost never did anymore. Deliberate silences formed a new trick that had crept into his arsenal. He was practicing the trick now. He had done the necessary, shown his identification. The other party should be a little rattled by now. He waited. Something might come up and, then again, it might not.

Wertheym had read the wording on Grijpstra's card and remembered his rank. "Cup of tea, adjutant? Or coffee? I was just going to have coffee myself."

"Please."

"Police," Wertheym said slowly. "*Po-lice*. First time I've been visited by a police officer, I think, doesn't happen in my trade. I just paint portraits, a harmless occupation. I've had the taxhounds after me but never the police. The taxman thought I hadn't been declaring my true income. Maybe I hadn't it, but he couldn't prove it so he went away again. So what have I done, adjutant?"

Grijpstra didn't have to answer. Wertheym had darted off but he came back again, carrying a tray with two flowered glasses. "Sorry, it's a bit of a mess in the kitchen. No cups today, but the coffee'll taste the same. Instant coffee, hope you don't mind, adjutant."

Grijpstra did mind.

"Mrs. Elaine Carnet," he said and sipped from the glass. "Does that name mean anything to you?"

"Yes. She is dead. Was in the paper this morning. And I painted her portrait, last year. She didn't model. I painted it from a poster, hell of a job it was. The poster was old and torn, a tear right through the face. A French poster. She used to sing in Paris, she said. I did the portraits and she paid cash and she left. Never saw her again. Nice woman, didn't quibble about the price—they often do, you know. Amazing, their vanity gets in the way of their greed, but I'm greedy too and I never drop my price. The hell with 'em, I always say. And if they argue, they'll pay in advance, all of it, or I won't touch the job.''

''Portraits?'' Grijpstra had moved and some coffee had spilled on his trousers. It was seeping through to his skin. He put the glass down and rubbed the stain. ''Portraits, you said? More than one, you mean?''

''Two portraits, identical—well, they differed a little, they were handmade, after all. She wanted two so I made two. Silly work, I mass-produced them. Little blob of blue on the one canvas, little blob of blue on the second canvas. I had never done that before, it was amusing in a way. It gave me ideas but nothing came of them. I specialize in female faces, you see, never do buildings or anything like that. If I could do buildings I could pick a particularly good one and do a whole series of them, just line up a lot of canvases and dance around, fill in the browns, then the reds, and so forth.''

''Yes.'' Grijpstra hadn't listened. ''So you did two portraits? Why?''

''I never ask why, adjutant. Why should I? Why should they want their portraits done anyway? There isn't one portrait I have done in the last ten years that I would want on my own wall. The ladies are all ugly as sin. I beautify them, of course, or I would have no business. In a way Mrs. Carnet's portrait was the best of them all: the poster showed her as a young woman. Young women aren't as ugly as old women.''

''Thank you,'' Grijpstra said. He left his almost full glass on the table. He had only taken two sips but the taste of the vile brew hung on in his mouth. He remembered that he had promised himself that this would be a good day. Fine, so he would find some real coffee somewhere. There were some pleasant sidewalk cafés in the vicinity. He would locate one and sit around for an hour and rid himself of the portrait painter's sickening fumes. There was plenty of time. Cardozo couldn't possibly be finished yet, he had been given a sizable job. He would make contact with Cardozo later and they could have more coffee while they thought of the right approach. They had to question Gabrielle Carnet again, and he didn't know what the suspect had answered to the commissaris's questions. Cardozo would have to fill him in. It would all take time. No hurry today.

His face looked placid as he ambled in the direction of the old city, careful not to hurt his toes against the uneven cobblestones and walking as close to the water of a narrow canal as the parked cars would permit. There had been a squall of rain, but the sun had come out again and now lit up a formation of seagulls patrolling the water for spoils and conversing raucously. A small boy was steering a homemade raft that was bumping crazily on the choppy waves in the wake of a barge.

He passed several cafés until he found one with the right conditions. It had a view of the canal, the waiter was an old man with a kind face, there was a fresh smell of coffee, and its terrace had already attracted several beautiful women. Fate seemed intent to disprove the portrait painter's harsh remark, for more beautiful women came just after Grijpstra had sat down. He looked around approvingly. An Oriental girl with a small finely chiseled face, long straight legs, and a tight bosom had draped herself in the opposite corner. Two blond girls, of that very light blond that originates in Scandinavian countries, were exposing their faces and a good portion of their bodies to the warming sun, and three black women, so stunningly well-shaped that they had to be models or ballet dancers, were talking to each other in the throaty melodious voices that he knew from de Gier's jazz records. He took in as much as he could stand and closed his eyes. The vision started almost immediately and he concentrated to hold it.

The six women were in a pond, set in a luscious tropical landscape. They were naked, of course. The Scandinavian and the Oriental girls were swimming, turning their lovely bodies through the clear water, the black ladies were climbing out, drops glistening on their ebony skin. There were rosebushes on the banks of the pond and beyond, a forest of fruit trees. The fruit trees didn't look right and changed into huge palms, their leaves rather similar to the commissaris's fern. Grijpstra himself was in the vision too, both as an objective substantial form and as an observer. He was riding a camel, circling the pond. The camel ride gave the adjutant the double pleasure of being able to look down into the pool and participating in the animal's sensuous sway. There was a close-up of the camel's feet sinking into high grass and lifting up again. A beautiful beast, incongruous to the scene but fitting all the same. The vision became more involved and less lusty. He noted many details in the girls' bodies, but they were of color and shape only and abstracted into a line play that got caught in the camel's slow dance. He smilingly drifted away into sleep when the commissaris entered the vision, running through the tall grass and waving.

The adjutant awoke and grunted. He left some change on the table and went into the café proper. There was a telephone.

"Ah, adjutant," the commissaris's secretary said in her grating voice. "I was waiting for your call. Cardozo has reported. He found witnesses to the attempt of dog poisoning and obtained statements. As we hadn't heard from you I told him to report for patrol duty, and he is with Sergeant Sietsema in a car now."

"No," Grijpstra said.

"Well, we can't let him hang around, can we? But I just had a message from the radio room. It appears that Cardozo forgot to check out a ring, he said you would know about it. The ring is on his desk and you'll have to go to the morgue with it." Grijpstra looked at the phone.

"Adjutant?"

He growled.

"And the commissaris and the sergeant have gone to the Pulitzer Hotel to talk with a Mr. Pullini, they will visit a Mr. Vleuten later today."

"Everything topsy-turvy as usual," Grijpstra said. "I need Cardozo to go and talk with Miss Carnet."

"Shall I get him back to headquarters, adjutant?"

"No. I'll take care of that damned ring first. I'll call you later." He slammed the phone down before remembering that this was going to be a good day.

"You can go back to bed if you like." There was a fatherly note of concern in the commissaris's voice. Francesco Pullini's almond-shaped dark eyes stared at the little old man unbelievingly.

"Police?"

"Yes, sir. Sergeant de Gier and I are police officers investigating the death of Elaine Carnet. May we sit down?"

Francesco gestured dumbly. He undid the knot of the tasseled belt around his dressing gown and tied it again. The commissaris and de Gier had sat down. The room in the Pulitzer Hotel was well furnished—it should be, at the price Pullini was paying. The room was quiet and spacious, high enough not to be bothered by the traffic murmuring below on the canal's narrow quay. An enormous double bed showed a slight dent where Francesco's slim body had been resting.

Francesco had had time to line up some thoughts. "Police, what for you come here?"

The commissaris didn't answer. He was observing the young man. His glasses reflected the sun so that a bright spot danced on Francesco's long, wavy, ink black hair.

De Gier was watching his suspect too. A female man, he had thought at first, but he remembered that Francesco was Italian and that Italians are daintier than the northern European male. There was some strength in the suspect's face, a well-shaped wide mouth and a good nose, straight and firm. The daintiness was mostly in the eyes, partly hidden by long lashes, and in the wave of the hair that touched the striped shoulders of the dressing gown. The door to the bathroom was open, and de Gier saw an array of jars and bottles and several leather cases, one of them would contain a hair dryer.

Francesco sat down. "What for you come see me, yes?" His naked feet crossed, high-arched dancer's feet; a thick mat of dark hair showed on his calves as he moved his legs.

"Mrs. Carnet's death," the commissaris said softly. "You must have heard, you visited the Carnet firm this morning, didn't you?"

Francesco's head came forward so that his hair fell and joined the carefully clipped beard, then shot up again. "Yes, I heard. Everybody very sad. Me, I also sad but, me, I don't know Madame Carnet well. My business always with Franco Bergen. Franco and me, us good friends. Madame Carnet, she somebody I say hello-how-are-you to. Kiss hand, give flowers, that all. What for police come see *me?*"

The commissaris's hands came up slowly and dropped back by their own weight. "Routine, Mr. Pullini. We are seeing everybody who knew Mrs. Carnet. You knew her."

"I knew her." Francesco jumped up from the bed and stood in the middle of the room with his arms spread, a miniature biblical prophet addressing the erring faithful. "So what? So does milkman, yes? Greengrocerman, yes? Man who cleans street?" He pushed an imaginary broom. "Morning, Madame Carnet. Nice day, Madame Carnet. You go and see cleaning man too? What is this, yes? Maybe you should leave this room, this my room."

Francesco was still pushing the broom. De Gier laughed and Francesco swung around, eyeballing the sergeant, poking the broom at him.

"Ha," de Gier said, and Francesco laughed too.

"You think I funny, yes?"

"Very funny, Mr. Pullini. Why don't you lie down? Are you ill?"

Francesco coughed, held his chest, and coughed again. "Yes, cold, the storm yesterday. Make me cough, so today I rest. Today I see Franco Bergen, maybe tomorrow I leave. In Milano much to do, I cannot wait forever for Bergen to change mind. Bah."

"The business isn't going well, Mr. Pullini?"

Francesco turned to face the commissaris. His right hand came up, balled, and made a turning movement. "Ehhhhh. Business, it always the same. Sometimes I screw Franco, sometimes Franco he screw me. Doesn't matter, we still friends. Same name, same character. His name Franciscus, my name Francesco."

"So you didn't know the Carnet family very well, did you, Mr. Pullini?"

Francesco was reading the card the commissaris had given him. "Commissaire, eh? You big shot?"

There was a friendly light in the Italian's liquid eyes and the commissaris responded. He balled his hand, turned it, and pulled up the corner of his mouth. "Ehhhhhhh."

Francesco smiled. "A drink!" There was a sly smile on the noble face. He reached for the telephone. "Gin, yes?"

"Orange juice," the commissaris said.

"One orange juice, two gin?"

"One gin, two orange juice."

The drinks came almost at once and Francesco squatted on the bed, toasting his guests.

"You were out last night and caught a cold?" The commissaris had gone back to his original concern. De Gier's eyes swept over the old man's face. An act again, of course, but he never knew how far the commissaris acted. What was an Italian's cold to the chief of Amsterdam's CID? But the commissaris was always concerned with the health of others and would regularly check the cell block at headquarters and sometimes made sure that prisoners were moved to one of the city's hospitals.

"I walk around, visit some bars, eat something, but then I come back, storm very bad. Cough."

"Did anyone see you come back, Mr. Pullini? The desk clerk? Do you remember who gave you your key? And the time of your return, perhaps?"

"I come back ten, ten-thirty, but I no ask for key. Key he in my pocket, forget to leave at desk, always forget." He pointed at the key on his night table. It was connected to a plastic bar that was only three inches long, it would fit into a pocket.

"Do you know Gabrielle Carnet, Mr. Pullini?"

"Sure." The sly smile moved the clipped beard again. "She nice girl, yes? I take her out once, twice maybe, not now, before. Now I married. Gabrielle, she know. Also bad business. Gabrielle, she daughter of *Madame* Carnet; Madame Carnet, she own Carnet and Company. Franco Bergen, he only owns little bit. He my friend, but he not say yes or no in end. Madame Carnet, she is God, yes? Maybe I better not play around with daughter of God."

"Really? I thought Madame Carnet wasn't very interested in her business anymore, that she was retired."

"Retired?"

"Yes, not work anymore?"

"I know word. Me, I know many words but I forget when I speak, I know when I hear. Madame Carnet, she not retired. She work, she chooses furniture, new models, she says to Franco Bergen 'not buy now, yes buy now.' She sometimes cut order in half. Me, I always get shits when Madame come in. First big order then . . . pfff!" He blew something off his hand. "Then nothing. I go back Milano and tell Papa 'no order,' then maybe order comes later but price is wrong. Low price. Madame Carnet, she clever."

"I believe Carnet and Company owes you some money, Mr. Pullini. Do you think you will get it before you go home?"

A slight tremor moved from the eyes and disappeared into Francesco's beard. "Money? You know, yes? Franco Bergen he tell you, yes?"

"We saw Mr. Bergen this morning. We have to ask questions, Mr. Pullini. A cigar?"

The commissaris got up and presented his flat tin. Francesco's hand moved to the tin but he pulled it back. "No, thank you, bad for cough. I bought cigarettes this morning, low tar, no taste, but something."

He lit a cigarette and puffed. "So you know about money. Yes. Franco Bergen, he no pay. He promise, but he no pay. This time Franco, he cat, me mouse. Little mouse, jump this way jump that way. Still no money."

"How much is involved, Mr. Pullini?"

Francesco held his hands about a meter apart. "In Italian so much." He brought his hands closer together "In Dutch so much."

"How much exactly?"

"Eighty thousand guilders. Sixteen million lire."

The sergeant whistled and Francesco imitated the whistle. He looked into de Gier's eyes but this time he didn't laugh.

"You were going to be given the money in cash?"

"Yes. Secret money. Goes into suitcase. But honest money, nothing to do with police. Pullini, he sells furniture; Franco Bergen, he pays cash. Bergen, he has invoices. All very nice."

"But you didn't get it."

"No. Franco Bergen he says he maybe buy from other firm in Milano, not from Pullini no more. When I say 'What about eighty thousand?' Bergen, he has dirty ears. So maybe I get lawyer, but that later. First I talk to Franco Bergen again. He old friend, he come to Milano, to Sesto San Giovanni where Pullini business is, he stays many weeks, he goes to mountains where Papa Pullini give him beautiful little house for month. Bergen, he bring family. Bergen, he eat in Pullini restaurant, no bill. Bergen, he remember. We talk some more."

"So you think Mr. Bergen will pay you?"

"Sure. Now he screw me but . . ."

"Good. I am glad to hear it, Mr. Pullini. Do you know where Madame and Gabrielle Carnet live?"

"Yes, before, I pick up Gabrielle. I remember street, Mierisstraat, nice street, big trees, maybe I can find street again."

"And you didn't find it last night?"

"No." Francesco coughed. The cough tore through his chest and he doubled up, holding his mouth into a handkerchief.

The commissaris waited for the attack to finish. They shook hands.

De Gier turned around in the corridor and caught the expression on Francesco's face as he closed the door.

"Well?" the commissaris asked in the elevator.

"A sad little man, sir, sad and worried, but he has a sense of humor."

"The sort of man who will push a lady down her own garden stairs?"

"No." De Gier was watching the little red-orange light of the elevator, jumping down, humming every time it hit the next glass button. "But a push doesn't take long. He is an excitable man and he wants his money. We may safely assume that the eighty thousand guilders are to be his, cash that he is lifting from his father's till. So he may be a little nervous about it."

"Sufficiently nervous to have pushed Mrs. Carnet last night?"

The commissaris shook his head, answering his own question. "No, I wouldn't think so. The amount may seem vast to us but to a businessman of Pullini's caliber it isn't all that much. Businessmen are usually very concerned about the continuation of their trade. Francesco will get his eighty thousand, now or later, but he won't get anything if he pushes his client to her death. No, I can't see it. Still . . ."

"Sir?"

The elevator's sliding door opened and they stepped into the hall and into a crowd of American tourists who had just been delivered by a bus and who were jockeying for position at the hotel's counter.

"You were saying, sir?" de Gier asked again as they

found each other under the striped awning of the hotel's entrance.

"Well, he might be lying. Or giving his version of the truth, which would also be lying. The truth is hard to catch. He has no alibi. He visited some bars. He walked around. So he says."

De Gier mumbled agreeably.

"Next!" The commissaris rubbed his hands. "The baboon's turn. This Mr. Vleuten may be a more interesting suspect. Had an affair with the lady and stepped out of it. Also stepped out of his job. He doesn't have to worry about any continuations for he broke his connection. He isn't expecting us, is he?"

"No, sir. I have his address, that's all. We can jump him the way we jumped Francesco just now."

They got into the car. "Jump him," the commissaris said. "I never know which attack is most effective. Sometimes it may be better to set up an appointment and let them work themselves into a cold sweat. But when we jump them they can't lie so easily." He picked up the microphone.

"CID here, headquarters?"

"Headquarters, sir."

"Any messages for me?"

"Yes, sir. Would you phone your secretary, please?"

The commissaris pushed the microphone back into its clip and got out again. De Gier waited behind the wheel.

"Yes, dear?"

"There was a call just now from Carnet and Company, sir, Miss Gabrielle Carnet, she left two messages. Mr. Bergen has become ill and went to see his doctor. It seems he has some facial paralysis that may be serious and he has gone to a hospital to see a specialist."

"That's bad, dear, but it was very nice of Miss Carnet to let us know. What else?"

"She said that her mother took out eighty thousand guilders in cash from the company's bank account yesterday, sir. Mr. Bergen found out this morning, after you and the sergeant left the Carnet office. He was very upset. Apparently it wasn't customary for Mrs. Carnet to deal with the bank directly. If she wanted anything Mr. Bergen would do the necessary. And Mr. Bergen remembered your saying that you had only found a few hundred guilders in Mrs. Carnet's safe last night.''

"Thank you, dear. How did Gabrielle Carnet sound?''

"Cool, sir. A businesslike sort of voice.''

"Well, well, well. How are Cardozo and Grijpstra doing? Weren't they supposed to visit Gabrielle? That won't be necessary now for Miss Carnet is at her office, they'll have to wait until this evening.''

"They are both out, sir. Cardozo has found witnesses to the dog poisoning and is now on street patrol, and Grijpstra is checking whether Mrs. Carnet's ring fits her finger tightly or not. He'll be in the morgue but he should be back shortly.''

"Ha." The commissaris rubbed his nose. "Ha. I think I'll be coming back to headquarters. Grijpstra can take over from me." As he walked back to the car he put out his left hand and said "Eighty thousand," then he put out his right hand and repeated the amount.

"Very simple," he added as he told his findings to de Gier. "Too simple, of course. But murder cases are simple sometimes. So suppose that Francesco went to see Elaine last night after all, and suppose he pushed her down the stairs and took her key from her purse and opened her safe. He did leave the household money, that was very decent of him.''

"Yes.''

"You don't sound very convinced, sergeant?''

"No, sir. We know now that Mrs. Carnet took out an amount identical to what her firm owed Francesco. Perhaps she took it out to give it to him. She may have taken it for a reason altogether detached from the case. The amount is big enough to buy a house, for instance, and I believe solicitors transacting real estate always demand payment in cash. According to Mr. Bergen, Mrs. Carnet wasn't interested in the day-to-day management of her company, maybe she didn't even know what her firm owed Francesco. But if she did know she must have taken the money to pay him, and if she meant to pay him there was no reason to kill and rob her.''

"True."

"But why would Mr. Bergen be suddenly suffering a facial paralysis, sir? Is he going to pieces because the police are questioning him?''

The commissaris grinned. "I knew you would say that, sergeant, and the conclusion isn't so far-fetched, but I think I know what is wrong with Mr. Bergen. I suffered from the same affliction some years ago. It is called Bell's palsy. I thought I had had a stroke and fussed and ran to a specialist, but it wasn't serious at all. An infection of the facial nerve: if the nerve doesn't work half the face becomes paralyzed, the eyelid won't close anymore, it becomes difficult to chew, and half the mouth droops, the way it does when you've been to the dentist. The paralysis wears off by itself, however, and the face becomes normal within a matter of weeks.''

"And what causes this palsy, sir? A nervous shock?''

"No, sergeant. A draft. I had been driving with an open window. Did you think the man was having a stroke?''

"Yes, sir."

"Maybe you were hoping that, eh, sergeant? Because you wanted to think that we had found our man.''

De Gier smiled apologetically.

They met Grijpstra in one of headquarters' corridors. The adjutant held up the wedding ring. "Not a very tight fit, sir, but not a very loose one, either. The corpse was almost frozen, so maybe the experiment was without value. When I left her, her arms were sticking straight up as if she couldn't bear my walking away. Brr. That morgue is a nasty place, sir. I saw at least ten bodies of young people dead of drug overdoses or malnutrition caused by drugs, and they were bringing in more as I left. The attendant said that they are mostly foreigners and all of them nameless and unclaimed.''

"Quite," the commissaris said gently. "Let's go to my office." Cardozo's report with the statements of the two old ladies was on his desk and he read it to the detectives.

"That sounds good enough, sir."

"Yes. Tell you what, sergeant, why don't you and the adjutant go and visit this baboon man now. I'll raise Cardozo on the radio and visit Mr. de Bree with him. Cardozo has done good work so far and a visit may lead to the fruition of his efforts."

They left the commissaris's office together and the detectives watched their chief march to the radio room, a dapper little figure in a long empty corridor.

"There he goes."

"There he goes. He seems a little fiercer than usual. What's bothering him, do you think?"

Grijpstra shrugged. "Let's catch that baboon."

They got into the old-fashioned elevator.

"Now where would this ape fit in?"

"Baboons are randy animals. The ones I have seen in the zoo were always either actually busy with or seemed to be thinking about it. He could represent the sexual aspect of this disorder."

"So could Francesco," de Gier said as they entered the garage. "A beautiful little Italian, they are very popular with our womenfolk."

Grijpstra wasn't listening.

"Baboons are dangerous too, he may rush us. Are you armed?"

"Of course. I'll drop him the minute I see his tail twitch."

They were both grinning when they got into the Volkswagen, but they were discussing lunch by then, and meanwhile, back in the morgue, Elaine Carnet's arms still reached for the ceiling while a grumbling attendant was trying to push her box back into the refrigerator.

9

Grijpstra's mouth opened foolishly as he watched the sergeant's body float elegantly through the fresh windswept air above the Amstel River, and it snapped shut as de Gier hit the river's greenish, garbage-littered surface and broke through it and disappeared. A disorganized swirl of bobbing objects remained. Grijpstra saw the bottletops, condoms, beer cans, and torn stems of waterweeds taking position in a more or less defined circle that moved to the quayside, and he cursed. Then he jumped. But he jumped away from the river and when he landed he ran. The Volkswagen wasn't too far off. The radio came on as he poked its button and the microphone's cord nearly broke as he yanked it free.

"Headquarters, Three-fourteen."

"Headquarters," the unperturbable female voice said.

"An emergency. We are on the Amsteldijk and a suspect has just got away in a motor launch. Could you locate the nearest water police vessel and connect me directly?"

"Understood. Wait."

Grijpstra counted. Eleven seconds. A very long time. He looked back at the river and saw the sergeant's head and one of his feet appear above the quayside. The head was crowned with a garland of waterweeds, the foot trailed an unidentified object attached, apparently, to some wire.

"Water police, what can we do for you?"

"Where are you?"

"Amstel River, about to go under the Thin Bridge, heading north."

"Turn around and go as far as the Berlaghe Bridge, stop on the northwest side, and we'll come aboard. Adjutant Grijpstra and Sergeant de Gier. Our suspect has got away in a white launch, going south."

"We can be at the Berlaghe Bridge in about five minutes."

"See you there. Out."

Five minutes, Grijpstra thought, an eternity. Anything can happen in five minutes. But a more cheerful thought interfered with his despair. The white launch had a fairly long stretch of river ahead, a stretch without any side escapes. They might just cut him off, the police boat would be faster than the old-fashioned launch. He slid into the Volkswagen and started its engine, which spluttered to life obediently. His stubby index finger pressed the siren into its first wail of terror. The Volkswagen's front tires squealed through a short U-turn and brought the car on a collision course with de Gier, who came running, leaving a trail of dripping slime.

Grijpstra leaned over and opened the passenger door.

"Shit," de Gier said as the car leaped off. "The bastard! Did you see what he did? He pushed the boat's gear forward and opened the throttle at the exact moment I jumped. I was lucky I fell free, I might have cracked my leg on his tiller."

"I saw it." Grijpstra grunted compassionately.

"And he was smiling, the bloody oaf. I know now why he is called the baboon. Did you see his face?"

Grijpstra had seen the face, split under the flat nose and the low forehead, split into a wide scowl of strong white teeth. The man did indeed look like an ape, a large powerful ape, but not a dangerous ape. Grijpstra's first impression had been quite positive. Yet what the suspect had just done belied the friendliness that Grijpstra had seen in the man's unusual, misshapen face.

The adjutant thought back as the Volkswagen careened through the Amsteldijk's traffic, overtaking cars that veered to the side as the siren howled on. De Gier had found a parking place right in front of Vleuten's house, a tall house, seven stories high, reaching for the overcast sky with the perfect double curve of its ornamental gable topped by a large plaster ball that in turn carried a spike. An ancient Rolls-Royce was parked half on the street, half on the sidewalk, and they had taken a minute to admire the vehicle before climbing the stone steps leading to the house's green-lacquered front door. De Gier was about to press the top bell, which said "Jan Vleuten," when a shout hailed them from the river and they had seen a man waving. The man stood on the cabin of an old-fashioned motor launch, painted bright white.

"I am Vleuten," the baboon shouted. "Do you want me?"

When they got to the launch the baboon stood near his tiller, holding the boat's painter, which had been swung around a large cleat on the quayside in a loose loop.

"Police," de Gier had said, squatting down to show his identification.

And while the baboon read de Gier's identification Grijpstra had formed his happy thoughts. A nice man, strange-looking for sure, but nice. And well dressed, in a thick white seaman's jersey that set off his wide chest. Light blond glossy hair caught under a small cap, the visor bent up. Long hair still showing the marks of a comb. Large calm blue eyes, very long arms that contrasted with the short legs. The body of an ape harboring the soul of an intelligent, kindly man. What had struck Grijpstra most, apart from the man's receding forehead and the absence of neck so that the head rested immediately on the potent torso, were Vleuten's arms. He remembered the large apes he had seen in the zoo and in films and how they walked, swinging, resting not only on their feet but equally on the knuckles of their hands. It seemed to him that Vleuten would walk the same way, and he was waiting for an opportunity to confirm his thought when de Gier's identification card was thrown onto the quay and the launch pulled away at full speed.

"Did you pick up your card?"

"Of course."

He still couldn't understand the suspect's response to their polite approach.

"Police?" The baboon had a good voice, deep and quiet.

"Yes, Mr. Vleuten. I am a CID sergeant. My colleague and I would like to ask a few questions."

The baboon had taken the card, a respectable weapon in their continuous warfare on crime—the police badge, the state's authorization decorated with the red, white, and blue of the flag of the Netherlands, an authorization that legalizes police officers to bother citizens, for their own sake, the sake of peace, and the maintenance of the rules of peace. And the fellow had actually had the audacity to throw the card on the street.

"You aren't worried about that damned card, are you?" de Gier asked. "What about me? Look at me!"

"You are wet," Grijpstra said pleasantly.

"Wet! I am probably poisoned. I swallowed some of that liquid shit they keep in the canals these days. I could have got killed on some of that garbage that floats around. I could have got drowned! You didn't even trouble yourself to see what had happened to me. All you were concerned about was your fucking radio."

"Now, now."

"But I still have my card, that's all the adjutant wants to know."

"You can swim," Grijpstra said, "and I would have worried about you but I saw you climbing out. And here we are."

"Where?"

"Here. I radioed a police boat. They're supposed to meet us here. Good, they're coming already, see?"

De Gier saw the gray speedboat pushing a fluffy bow wave but he didn't seem interested. He looked down at his hands and began to wipe them. His right hand had bled a little; the left hand had a long gluey yellow weed stuck between the fingers. He pulled it out and threw it out of the window.

"He took a risk," the adjutant said, forcing the car to take a short turn to the right and to dive under a large bridge, Amsterdam's main thoroughfare, connecting its center to the eastern part of the city. They could hear the bridge's rumble as a convoy of trucks passed overhead. "I could have shot him easily, but only in the chest or the head. His legs were covered by his boat's gunwale. Maybe he knows that we only aim for the legs, provided they are not actually attacking us."

De Gier was wringing out his trouser legs. "That's my second suit today, got it from the dry cleaner's this morning. We'll have to catch him, Grijpstra. I want him in a cell, a bad cell, the corner cell." The police launch was waiting and they jumped in, ignoring the water sergeant's helpful arm.

"CID, sergeant, go south, we are after a white motorboat, one man in it, man with a white jersey and a cap. A good-looking boat, old but well kept. A wooden boat."

The constable in the launch's cabin shifted a small lever next to the steering wheel. The boat roared and began to cut through the river's short bright waves, lifting its nose as it gathered speed. Grijpstra stumbled, but the water sergeant caught him by the shoulders.

"Hold on, your friend took a bath, did he?"

"He did. The suspect removed his boat as my colleague jumped."

Hands were shaken as the policemen introduced themselves.

"What's the chase, Grijpstra? Is your suspect dangerous? Armed?"

Grijpstra explained. De Gier had gone into the cabin and was checking his pistol, breaking it into parts and drying it with a rag. The constable gave him a fresh clip and de Gier inserted it. "It'll work," the constable said, "but you'd better take it to the arms room, there are a lot of little bits and pieces that'll rust eventually. You plan to shoot your man, sergeant?''

"I'd love to but I wouldn't be thanked if I did. I don't even know why he got away."

"You have a charge against him?"

"He used to sleep with a lady we know."

The constable wasn't listening anymore. A towboat had appeared, tugging asthmatically at a line of three gigantic barges. The barges were following unsteadily and the racing police-launch seemed to be attracted by the last vessel's looming, rusty hull. The little lever on the dashboard was pushed further and the boat's engines roared a shade deeper.

"Missed her," the constable said. "That's a charge, sergeant? Sleeping with a lady you know?"

"The lady is dead. We're going around asking questions."

"And you land up in the river. Happened to me too. I was shoved off an ocean liner's gangway last week. Part of the job. We keep dry clothes in that cupboard. Maybe they'll fit you. A sergeant's uniform. It'll fit your rank if not your body."

The river was clear, and the constable relaxed and watched de Gier strip. "There's a towel in there too, and underwear, and I have a pair of rubber boots here somewhere. We keep everything, even a small machine gun I can mount on the foredeck. There's something wrong with the gun's breech but it looks most impressive." De Gier stepped into the boots. "No, thanks, I don't think our man is armed. How do I look, constable?"

The water sergeant and Grijpstra had come into the cabin and de Gier was admired. The uniform fitted.

"Stunning," Grijpstra said. "I prefer the gold trim to our silver. Why do the water police have gold trim anyway?"

"Because gold is noble and so are we," the water sergeant said. "The water may be polluted these days, but it can never be as dirty as the shore."

The sun had found an opening in the low clouds above the city and the river's wide expanse, dotted here and there by the spotless white of floating sea gulls spread all around them. The launch was skimming over the short waves. The water sergeant unscrewed the top of a large thermos. "Fresh coffee, made less than half an hour ago." The four men were grinning as the baboon's boat showed up as a speck near the next bend of the river. "Not a bad life, this," the water sergeant said, pouring the coffee. "I don't know why you chaps prefer to work in the city. Narrow streets, no air, people everywhere. The people are the worst, they always want something."

"Don't you deal with people?" Grijpstra asked.

"Sometimes, but I usually manage to avoid them. I prefer fish. We do a fair bit of fishing, you know. And there are always the birds. Some of the birds are stupid, especially the ducks, but I would still rather deal with ducks than with people. People, bah!"

Grijpstra looked up. "What happened to that boat? It was right in front of us just now."

The constable pointed and turned the wheel at the same time, making the police boat knife through the river's curve. "Over there, moored to the jetty. That's the baboon's launch, I thought I recognized it before but I wasn't sure. Is the baboon your suspect?"

"Yes. You know him evidently."

The water sergeant had stepped to the dashboard and turned the key, cutting the boat's engines so that it settled back into the water. "Yes, Grijpstra, we know the baboon, everybody on the water does. But he doesn't seem to be on board."

"Never mind, go back a little and drop us off on the dike, out of sight of the jetty if possible. It could be that he hasn't spotted us. We can sniff around a little. If we don't catch him today we'll catch him tomorrow."

"Sleuths," the water sergeant said to his constable. "Intelligent hunting hounds. I hope you are observing and learning. We would just go away and take that old boat with us but we don't have brains. Sure, the suspect will come back to his boat and walk into our friends' arms." He turned back to Grijpstra. "Are you certain he's your man?''

"Shouldn't he be?''

"No. Tell me again why you're after him.''

Grijpstra wrinkled his nose; he appeared to be lifting something heavy on his flat hands. "We know we are after him but we don't know why exactly. He made my sergeant leap into the river, that's one reason. And he used to sleep with a lady named Elaine Carnet and the lady died under suspicious circumstances. We went after him to ask some questions, routine questions, and he didn't give us a chance to ask them. He took off.''

"He's a good man.'' The water sergeant's eyes seemed to be pleading. "I've known him for a few years now, on the water and in a few pubs. He is an artist in a way, restoring our part of the world. The baboon finds old boats, wrecks, there are plenty of them around, rotting and forgotten. He buys and repairs them. Some old men are working with him, retired men who have nothing to do. The baboon got them interested in living again. The municipality is interested in what he's trying to do. They've given him the use of a small city wharf up north. The old men are very proud of their work. They don't work for money, but the baboon sees to it that they get something, and when a boat is in good order again he will sell it at a fair price to somebody he thinks will appreciate a good boat.''

"He does? Does he own that old Rolls we saw parked in front of his address?''

"Yes. Same story. Bought as a wreck, taken apart, and reassembled. Same with his house too. I believe he inherited the house, but it was in poor shape, and he remodeled it completely and lets the six lower stories at reasonable rents. He could be a shark, most house owners are, but he isn't.''

Grijpstra was listening intently, softly scratching around in his bristly short hair. De Gier, resplendent in his dark blue uniform, was listening too.

"You hear that?'' Grijpstra asked.

"I heard, but I still have some weeds in my ears, so maybe I didn't hear it all. A latter-day saint, eh? So why did this lovable gentleman who looks like an ape make me take a flying leap at the river? I wasn't hustling him, was I? He barely gave me time to state my purpose, then whoosh . . . him away and me . . . In fact, I may have a charge for attempted manslaughter against him, or trying to cause serious injury. What else do you know about him? Nothing bad at all?"

"No. I have no idea why he took off, but I know that if you bother him you'll have everybody against you, everybody out here, the people of the waterways."

The launch rubbed itself against the quayside and Grijpstra held on to a tree stump.

"Give us a push, sergeant. We won't harm your hero, unless we can prove you wrong, and even then we wouldn't be too nasty."

De Gier jumped out too. "Thanks for the assistance, you'll have your uniform back in the morning. I'll try to keep it clean, but maybe your friend will have me in the river again."

The water sergeant grinned. "Not in that uniform, he'll respect the gold."

The launch backed away and the two officers waved. It took the detectives a few minutes to walk to the jetty. The baboon had tied up his launch neatly but he wasn't around.

"You want to snoop around here a bit?"

"May as well."

But they were ready to give up and catch a tram back to their car when Grijpstra suddenly whistled. "Over there, on the terrace."

The baboon was peacefully drinking tea. They stopped in front of his table.

"Afternoon, Mr. Vleuten."

The baboon smiled as if welcoming old friends. "Well, I never. And in a water cop's uniform too. Would you join me?"

They sat down but they didn't say anything, and the silence, awkward at first, lost its tension as the three men gazed at the river. De Gier took off his cap and put it on the table and a girl came and took their order.

"I hope you didn't hurt yourself," the baboon said and offered a cigarette.

"I did."

"Badly?"

"No. A scratch. But I did get very wet and dirty."

The baboon touched de Gier's shoulder. "I'm sorry. You came to see me about the fine, did you? I won't pay it."

"Fine?"

"Yes."

"I didn't come to see you about a fine, we came to ask you some questions. A Mrs. Carnet died. Elaine Carnet. We were told you knew her."

"Ah." The baboon sighed. "I might have known. I read about Elaine's death but the journalist said it was an accident. Wasn't it?"

"Perhaps. What is this business about a fine, Mr. Vleuten?"

"Call me baboon. I don't like the word but it has stuck to me for a long time. That fine is a conglomeration of parking fines. Some parking police constable is irritated by my Rolls-Royce, he goes out of his way to plaster tickets all over it. I've complained to his chief but nothing happens. I don't mind paying an occasional fine like everybody else, but I'm damned if I'll have one every day. There aren't enough parking places in the city and I have a car, so have a hundred thousand others."

"But why associate us with your fines?"

"I've been bothered by you before, not by you personally, but by detectives. They keep ringing my bell in the early morning and shouting at me through the microphone at the front door."

"Different branch, you must be referring to personnel from the court. They will be after you to try and get you to the court's cashier and they have powers to hold you until you pay—if you open your door to them, that is. They aren't authorized to break it down or to grab you in the street. They'll have to take you from your house and you have to be willing to be taken."

"I am not."

De Gier was watching the baboon's calm face. "You might be in trouble now, you know. You made me suffer a bad fall."

"Can you arrest me?"

"Yes."

"Will you?"

"Not just now. But we'll have to question you. Where do you want to be questioned? Here?"

They had finished their tea and the baboon called the girl and paid. "No, not here. And I am sorry about your fall. I thought you were sent by the parking police and I feel badly about this nonsense. A misunderstanding. I apologize, do you accept?"

De Gier nodded. "Maybe I will."

"Then be my guests a little longer, gentlemen. We can take the boat back to my house and you can question me there, but I may not have much to say. I had no reason to kill Elaine, and I wouldn't have killed her if I'd had a reason. Maybe there's never a reason to kill, except to avoid old age, and Elaine wasn't old."

Grijpstra felt the little hairs in his neck bristle. He had detected the tremendous strength that seemed to come out of the baboon's being, waves of strength that enveloped the detectives and neutralized their own force. Grijpstra remembered other occasions when he had been almost hypnotized by suspects. He had felt it during some arrests and also, once or twice, when he had been a witness for the prosecution in court. He had seen high police officers, lawyers, judges even, wilt while an unruffled criminal pleaded his case, made statements, proved himself to be innocent. But the criminals had been guilty.

They ambled across the quay together and de Gier lowered himself carefully into the launch. He was looking at some rubbish floating under the jetty as the baboon started the launch's engine.

"Bah," de Gier said. "Look at that mess. That water sergeant is a chauvinist. His part of the world is dirtier than ours."

The baboon looked too. "We're making an effort. The

river is getting cleaner, it was much worse before."

"Bah. People used to swim in the river."

"They will again."

"I was swimming in it just now."

The baboon laughed. "I said I was sorry."

"Sure," de Gier said. "That was very nice of you."

10

"He isn't in," the square lady in the flowered dress said, "but he's due back any moment. Could you come again in half an hour, perhaps?"

The commissaris and Cardozo had stood for quite a while on the porch of the de Bree house while Mrs. de Bree peered at them through the door's peephole and tried to make up her mind whether or not to open the door. She had seen Cardozo before and knew he was a policeman. Her husband had told her not to let in the police. But the other man was much older than the boyish detective, and he didn't seem to be the sort of man who could be sent away. She had decided that the commissaris looked, in an unobtrusive way, both dignified and intelligent, and she had taken the risk. But now she was stuck again.

"We won't go away, Mrs. de Bree," the commissaris said softly, "and you will have to let us in."

"My husband says that the home is private and that . . ."

"The home is private, your husband is right."

She faltered and blushed. "So . . . ?"

"But there are exceptions to any rule, madame. A crime has been committed and the police have been asked to investigate. In such circumstances the police have the right to enter any dwelling by force if a warrant has been issued or if an officer of a certain rank wants to visit the home."

"I see." She didn't want to ask for the commissaris's rank, but he had given her a card and she glanced at it. She didn't know anything about police ranks. "Well, would you come in then, please. I hope you'll explain to my husband when he comes . . ."

"We will."

Cardozo stepped aside and the commissaris marched into the corridor and waited for Mrs. de Bree to lead the way. They were taken to a room in the rear of the house, similar to the enclosed porch in the Carnet house. Evidently the same architect had been used for all the homes in the two streets sharing the enclosed garden area. Mrs. de Bree offered tea and gratefully retired to the kitchen.

Cardozo jumped out of his chair the minute they were alone. "My witnesses live over there, sir. They have the top floor of the house, there with the balcony, behind the geraniums. Two old ladies with binoculars, ideal witnesses, they have a full view of both this garden and the Carnet garden opposite. And there's the liguster hedge and Mr. de Bree must have stood next to that rhododendron bush when he fed Paul. With binoculars my witnesses could have seen that he was feeding him chopped meat. With the laboratory test that proves that there was both chopped meat and arsenic in Paul's stomach, and with the matching times of the witnesses' statements and Gabrielle Carnet's complaint plus the statement of the veterinarian we have an airtight case against de Bree."

The commissaris had come to the window. "Yes, good work, Cardozo. I wonder if I can smoke here. Does de Bree smoke?"

Cardozo looked around. "There's a pipe rack on the wall, sir, and several ashtrays."

"Then I'm sure Mrs. de Bree won't mind. Hey!"

A cat had landed on the balcony outside. It had dropped from a tree branch with such a thud that Cardozo, who was still studying the pipe rack, had turned around. The cat was oversize, not only fat but enormous in proportions. A lynx with tufted ears, with thick fur spotted with black and orange and with a cruel square head, bright orange on one side, deep black on the other. The line dividing the two colors didn't run in the exact middle of the face, shortening the black half slightly, with the result that his expression was startlingly weird.

"That's a cat, sir?"

"I think so. But perhaps it has a small panther or an ocelot as an ancestor, although I do believe that some breeds of domesticated cats grow rather large. All of twenty pounds, I would say, more perhaps."

The cat walked to the window and stood up, pressing its face and front paws against the glass. The soles of its feet were heavily haired.

"It's purring," the commissaris said. "Perhaps it means well. Should we let it in, Cardozo?"

Mrs. de Bree was with them again, carrying a tray. "Ah, Tobias. Would you mind opening the door, sir? Poor thing must be hungry. He probably tried to come in before but I was vacuum-cleaning upstairs and didn't hear him. He's been out all morning."

The commissaris released the door's latch and Tobias rushed in, forcing the door out of his hand. He ran across the room and loped off into the corridor.

"An amazing animal, madame. Very big, isn't he?"

"Yes. But he's getting old and is blind in one eye now and not too well. We had him operated on for cancer last year and he recovered, but the vet says that the cancer may still be there and that a second operation wouldn't do any good. My husband is very upset about it. Tobias is like a child and we have had him fourteen years—we don't have any real children, you see. And Tobias is so clever!"

The commissaris stirred his tea. The room was pleasant and quiet; there was no sound in the house except a rattling in the kitchen where Tobias was gulping his food and pushing its container around.

"You know why we came, don't you, Mrs. de Bree?"

She was sitting unnaturally upright and playing with a lace handkerchief. There were tears in her mild eyes, enlarged by the thick lenses of her gold-rimmed spectacles.

"Yes, sir, you came about Paul. I'm so saddened about that. I don't know what got into my husband, he's never done anything like that before. He won't admit what he did to Paul, but he knows that I know. He hasn't talked to me much since it happened. And the old ladies opposite saw him do it, Alice came to see me about it an hour ago. She said they had told the police and that they were sorry but they couldn't help it, so I was expecting you, you see."

"What does your husband do, Mrs. de Bree?"

"He's retired in a way. He's an engineer and has invented things, we have an income from royalties. Sometimes I wish he were still working."

They heard a key turn in the front of the house and Mrs. de Bree jumped up and rushed into the corridor, shutting the door behind her. The conversation took a full five minutes and de Bree's voice gradually lost its anger. Mrs. de Bree was crying. He came in alone.

"Mr. de Bree?"

The policemen were on their feet. De Bree pointed at their chairs and thought of something to say. Tobias was bumping the door. "My cat, I'll let him in."

De Bree sat down, he sighed, and all the air appeared to go out of him. The sigh seemed endless.

"I'm sorry," the commissaris said. "But what has to be done has to be done, sir. You weren't getting anywhere when you refused my detective entry, surely you knew that, didn't you?"

"Are you arresting me?"

"No."

De Bree reached for his pipe rack and tobacco tin. The tobacco spilled as his trembling hands tried to fill the pipe. He couldn't find a match and looked about helplessly. The commissaris gave him his lighter.

"So why did you come?" de Bree asked between puffs.

"To obtain your confession, sir. It isn't strictly needed, the evidence against you is conclusive, but a confession might help you, the judge will be better disposed."

"Judge? You'll make me go to court?"

"Yes."

Tobias walked past de Bree's chair and de Bree grabbed the cat's tail. It closed with strength and the cat pulled, finding support in the carpet. De Bree's chair moved an inch but stuck on the carpet's edge. The cat looked around, turned, and put a paw on de Bree's hand. It purred and its good eye opened until it was a large shiny green disk. De Bree grunted and released the tail.

"He must be very fond of you," the commissaris said. "His nails didn't come out."

"He'll never scratch me. He did once, by mistake, and drew blood and he was sorry for a week. He followed me everywhere I went. He loves me, he even hunts for me. He is always bringing me birds and mice, rats even. Once he caught a crow, a big crow. Crows are hard to catch. He brought the bird to my bed, I was ill at the time, and dropped it on the blanket. Made a mess, my wife didn't like that, but he loves her too."

"You like animals, don't you?"

"I like Tobias. I don't get on with other animals, or with people. My wife and I live very much on our own, but we don't mind. If they don't bother us we don't bother them. I have my books. I am an engineer. I have a basement where I can work. I don't need anybody anymore."

The commissaris had been looking at a large framed painting hanging in the shadows of the room.

"That's Tobias," de Bree said. "My wife did it. It isn't painted but embroidered, in very small stitches. We found a store where an artist will do a portrait on canvas and they sell you wool so that you can embroider the portrait yourself. People usually like to make portraits like that of their children but we don't have any. I gave my wife the canvas for her birthday. It took her months to stitch it."

The commissaris had got up to study the gobelin. "Remarkable! An amazing likeness. Your cat has an interesting face."

Cardozo whipped out his handkerchief and began to blow his nose furiously.

De Bree had lost interest. He was staring at the floor, his hand resting limply on the cat's back.

"I'm sorry," he said. "Does that help? If I say I am sorry? I'll pay if you like. The Carnet ladies must have had some expenses, perhaps they want to put in a claim. I'll pay for the vet and whatever you say I should pay on top of the vet's bill for damages. I suppose I owe it to them."

"The judge would like to hear you say that." The commissaris had sat down and was stirring his tea. "But why did you want to kill Paul? Death through arsenic poisoning is very unpleasant, painful. The victim suffers cramps, vomits, he may suffer for a fairly long time until the coma finally sets in. You knew that, didn't you?"

"Yes, I suppose so. I didn't think of it. Arsenic is the only poison I could find, they sell it to kill rats. I would have bought a better poison if it had been available."

"But why kill the dog?"

De Bree shrugged. "There was no choice. Paul is a young strong dog. Terriers are fierce and quick on their feet. So is Tobias, but Tobias can only see on one side. The silly cat doesn't know that the gardens around belong to others, he thinks they are all his private hunting ground. The other cats run away when they see him coming but Paul is a hunter too, and he has been out to kill Tobias for a while now. I have broken up some of their fights, but I can't be in the garden all the time. So . . ."

"No." The commissaris had put down his cup and his hands grabbed the sides of his chair. "No, sir. You should have thought of another solution. A very high fence, for instance, there's a limit to what cats can do. A carpenter could have constructed a fence that couldn't have been scaled by Tobias. The point is that you didn't want to restrict your cat. You can't deny other people the right to have a pet because their pet is a threat to yours. You could also have moved to the country. You are not economically bound to the city. You have alternatives, Mr. de Bree."

De Bree's eyelids sagged. "I said I was sorry."

"Yes."

Cardozo had brought out his notebook. "I'll have to take your statement, sir. Would you describe what you did and tell us exactly when you did it. It can be a short statement, but it'll have to be in your own words."

"On Wednesday, the first of June, at about twelve hundred hours . . ."

De Bree's voice was flat. Cardozo was writing furiously as the voice droned on. De Bree proved that his mind was trained in exactitude and had the ability to report logically connected events.

Cardozo read the statement back and de Bree brought out his fountain pen.

"Thank you," the commissaris said, "and please thank your wife for her hospitality."

"Will I have to go to jail?" de Bree asked as the policemen stepped into the street.

"It's up to the judge, sir. I'm sorry, our task is finished now. Perhaps you should consult your lawyer when you receive the summons."

The door closed with an almost inaudible click.

"A telephone, Cardozo. Is there a public booth around?"

"Any news, dear?"

He held the phone away from his ear as his secretary reported.

"Grijpstra and the sergeant had some trouble, sir. The radio room says that they had to ask the water police for assistance. I've had a report from the water police too, but it isn't very detailed. It only says that they chased a boat belonging to a Mr. Vleuten and that Mr. Vleuten wasn't with his boat when they found it. Sergeant de Gier fell into the river somewhere along the chase but he wasn't harmed."

"Really?"

"Yes, sir. And I've had a call from Gabrielle Carnet, she found a hundred thousand guilders under her mother's mattress and thought you would like to hear about it."

"I would, yes. Anything else? Any news about Mr. Bergen and his facial trouble?"

"Yes, sir, I asked Miss Carnet. The hospital referred Mr. Bergen to a private neurologist and the neurologist detected some serious trouble, it seems. Mr. Bergen will have further tests tomorrow. He is at home now, I have the address. He telephoned his office and Miss Carnet was there when the call came in.''

The commissaris wrote down the address and telephone number, fumbling on the small metal desk provided in the booth, and managed to drop his ball-point and bump his head as he came up again.

''Oh, sir.''

''Yes?'' He had dropped his ball-point again and was rubbing his head.

''There was a note on your desk that I don't think you've seen. It was brought up from Grijpstra's room as it was addressed to you. A report on the adjutant's visit to a portrait painter called Wertheym?''

''Yes. Go on.''

''It only says that Wertheym made two identical portraits for Mrs. Carnet. The 'two' is underlined.''

''Thanks.'' He hung up. Cardozo was staring at him foolishly, his nose pressed against the glass of the booth. The commissaris opened the door, slamming it into Cardozo's arm. ''Don't stand there like an idiot, Cardozo, did I hurt you?''

''No, sir.''

''Your friend the sergeant got himself into the Amstel River this afternoon, something to do with chasing the baboon, apparently. I wish they'd phoned in. I've no idea where they are now, looks as if I'll have to run after my own assistants. My own fault. I'm pushing this case too hard.''

They walked back to the car. The neighborhood was experiencing a short burst of liveliness as heads of families were coming home, welcomed by grateful wives. Everywhere around them car doors slammed, children rushed out of front doors, fathers put down their briefcases to embrace their offspring. The late afternoon sun was pouring a thick, diffuse light into the long, tree-lined street so that each object threw a tapered, clearcut shadow.

The commissaris stopped to admire a creeper, heavily studded with clusters of white flowers, that had covered an entire wall and seemed ready to climb over it. ''Beautiful. But we are still stuck, Cardozo. Remember that motive that was thrown at us? Mrs. Carnet's eighty thousand guilders? Taken from the bank yesterday, in cash, in crisp notes? Nowhere to be found now?''

"Yes, sir, you told me."

"Well, it grew to a hundred thousand and it has shown up again, under the lady's mattress. Gabrielle found the money and was good enough to phone my office. Back where we started."

Cardozo, who had been nodding encouragingly, lost his smile. He looked so crestfallen that the commissaris cheered up again. "Never mind. Good luck comes to those who keep on trying. The old chief constable used to say that and he was right. Tell you what, Cardozo, you go to see Gabrielle now, she's around the corner. Find out the details of the lucky find and phone your report to the radio room. You can go home afterward, perhaps you should stay home. If I manage to find the adjutant and the sergeant I'll contact you and we may have a conference to finish off the day."

Cardozo almost came to attention, turned around, and marched down the street. The small figure in its shabby corduroy jacket, bouncing under a mop of curly hair, looked incongruous between the elegant houses. The commissaris nodded approvingly. Cardozo's willingness to do his share showed. The young man was shaping up well, but he wasn't a complete policeman yet. The commissaris remembered words spoken by his superiors, who had, since then, turned into old men and doddered into their graves. A policeman is cunning but moderate. Sly as a snake, innocent as a dove. He said the word aloud. "Sly." A good word. To be sly without malice. He would need his slyness now, to sort out this mess caused by uncontrolled but very human emotions. A poisoned dog and a clownish, frumped-up woman, dead in a pool of rainwater. He wondered what else they would find, for the emotions weren't curbed yet. He knew that his main task was to prevent further manifestations and he would have to solve the present riddle to be able to do so.

A large white motorcycle whizzed past, ridden by what

looked to be a mechanical man, completely wrapped in white leather, his face hidden by a plastic visor. The Amsterdam police emblem, a naked sword resting on an open book, was painted on the motorcycle's metal saddlebag. It also showed on the policeman's helmet. The motorcycle's presence kept drivers in line. The commissaris looked at his own image mirrored in a store window. The image peered back at him, a small man dressed in grays with a thin face and a glint of gold-rimmed spectacles. Chief of the murder brigade, gliding through the city almost transparent, completely unnoticed. "A sneak," he said aloud. What could a sneak prevent? But he would do his best, his very best, and his mind was locked on the case again as he opened the door of the Citroën.

11

The commissaris pointed the sleek nose of the Citroën away
from the curb and waited patiently for an opening. He sat
poised at the wheel. The opening came and the car lurched
forward and immediately lost the impact of its leap as it
settled sedately, nudged into the homeward stream. The
commissaris grinned at the success of his maneuver, but
the grin faded away as pain activated the nerves in his
thighs. He knew he should be home in bed, with his tube
of medication on the night table and his wife hovering
around, speaking to him soothingly, fluffing up his cushions, caring. The radio crackled.

"Commissaris?"

"Yes."

"The adjutant has telephoned, sir. They found their suspect, Mr. Vleuten, and are now on the river in the suspect's
boat. The interrogation will take place at Mr. Vleuten's
house, Amsteldijk One-seven-two."

"Thank you, I'll go there now."

"Do you want your secretary to stay in your office, sir?"

"No. Thank her for her assistance. Over and out."

He was almost home, but he took the first road on the
left and headed for the river. To be driving around, straining

himself, pushing a case that could just as well be solved by his assistants, was pure idiocy. Or sanity, if his choice was between activity and the slow senseless existence of some delicate plant in a greenhouse. He had been ill for a long time now, with no real hope of recovery, although he kept trying to convince his wife of the opposite. Activity might kill him, but it would keep him alert meanwhile.

The car shot through an orange light, turned again, and began to follow the river. He glanced at the house numbers; another block to go. He found the mooring and parked under a row of elms that had survived the gale. The pain in his thighs had reached a steady level and he could bear with it. He got out, content to wait. A tanker came chugging up the river and he admired its strong sturdy lines under the superstructure of artfully intertwined tubes painted a brilliant white. He leaned against a tree and returned the tanker's greeting, a slow solemn wave of the man at the wheel. A heron, balanced on a partly submerged log saw the commissaris's arm move and lifted a long leg but decided to stay where it was and pointed its beak at the water again. Some fat coots were rowing about busily, only a few yards away, headed for a patch of duckweed, rippling in the river's flow. The commissaris was still leaning against the elm when the baboon's boat arrived and touched the quayside with a tire hung over its gunwale.

An ape man, definitely, the commissaris thought as he watched Vleuten move the tiller. De Gier was standing next to the suspect; the baboon's golden mane stood out against the sergeant's uniform. The commissaris caught the rope thrown by Grijpstra and held it while he waited for the three men to join him.

"Mr. Vleuten, sir. Mr. Vleuten, please meet our chief."

They shook hands and crossed the street in pairs, Grijpstra and the baboon going ahead.

"Have you arrested him, de Gier?"

"No, sir. He has been very well behaved."

"The radio room says that you fell into the river. If that event was caused by your suspect an arrest would be warranted."

De Gier explained and the commissaris nodded. "Good. No vengeance."

The commissaris thought back. He was a young inspector again, long ago, thirty years ago. He had been beaten up by a suspect and the suspect was subsequently caught. When he went to the station a constable had taken him down to the cell block where his man was chained to a pipe, cowering. The constable had told him to go ahead and had turned and left the basement. He had been tempted, but he had released the suspect and taken him to a cell and gone upstairs.

"No vengeance," he said again. "That's very good, de Gier."

Some surprise showed on the sergeant's face. "I thought it would be better not to ruffle him, sir. This way he may talk easier."

"You'll lay charges against him later?"

De Gier looked uncomfortable. "I can't, sir. I more or less accepted his apology. A case of mistaken identity, really, he mistook me for an officer from the court. He has some parking fines he has been protesting and the court constables have been bothering him."

"Good. Is this our man's house?"

"Yes, sir, and that's his car."

The commissaris took a moment to observe the seventeenth-century house and the Rolls-Royce.

"A nineteen thirty-six model I would say, sergeant, but very well kept. It should be worth some money, and the house is very valuable, of course. So he isn't badly off, your baboon. That would explain why he resigned so easily from Carnet and Company. Still, he did refuse unemployment benefits, Mr. Bergen told me. Most unusual. He would qualify and they are eighty percent of previous income and will be paid for several years now, I believe. And he turned it down. Most unusual."

The baboon had opened the door and gone in with Grijpstra, and the commissaris and the sergeant began to climb the stairs slowly, pausing on the landings. Even so the commissaris was exhausted when they finally reached the seventh floor. The baboon's apartment was open and the commissaris sunk into the first chair he saw. The baboon was busying himself at the kitchen counter.

Grijpstra looked at the commissaris. "Do you want to ask the questions, sir?"

The commissaris shook his head. He had closed his eyes, his breath was still coming in gasps. "Go ahead, adjutant."

The baboon served coffee and sat down. "Gentlemen?"

Grijpstra phrased his questions slowly and precisely and the baboon's answers connected promptly.

"Yes, I visited her last night, early in the evening."

"Why, Mr. Vleuten?"

"To repay a loan. I shouldn't have borrowed from her but I didn't want to increase my mortgage on the house. The bank has always been very helpful, it's the same bank Carnet and Company uses and I know the manager well, but even so, mortgages take time and I needed money promptly. I had miscalculated on the remodeling costs of two of the apartments below and the workmen expected to be paid, of course. In a weak moment I asked Elaine to lend the cash to me, that was six months ago. Since then I sold a boat and made some money again, so last night I took the money to her."

"How much?"

"Twenty thousand. She gave me the money in cash and I returned it in cash. She didn't ask for interest. I've often done repairs in her house and I never charged her and I think she wanted to repay the favor."

"You have a receipt, sir?"

"No. It was a loan between friends."

"Were you seeing her regularly?"

"No, not anymore. I hadn't seen her since she lent me the money, and that was half a year ago, as I said."

"Was she expecting you?"

"No."

"Did you have the impression that she was expecting anybody else?"

The baboon got up and stretched. The three policemen looked at the short legs that dwarfed the man; when he dropped his arms they swung loosely.

"Yes, she was very well dressed, overdressed, I would say. At first I thought she was planning to go out and I asked her where she was going. She said she wasn't going anywhere."

"Did she seem nervous?"

"Yes. I thought it was the gale. It was a strange night, the gale had already started up. She talked a good deal, but she didn't exactly make me welcome."

"Did she offer you anything? A drink?"

"No."

"Do you smoke, Mr. Vleuten?"

"I'm trying to give it up. I have cigarettes here but I don't carry them anymore. I only smoke when I have to, about ten cigarettes a day now."

"So you didn't smoke while you were with Mrs. Carnet last night?"

"No."

The commissaris was following the conversation but the words seemed far away; his breathing had slowed down and he was controlling the pain. He noticed that the baboon wasn't asking Grijpstra to explain his questions. He forced himself to sit up and observe the suspect. The baboon's and the commissaris's eyes met for an instant. There was a slight gleam in the man's eyes. He seemed amused but there was also sadness, mainly in the lines of the wide lips.

"What time did you leave?"

"Around eight. I only stayed a quarter of an hour, I think."

Grijpstra sat back and the commissaris raised a hand. "Your money was found, Mr. Vleuten. I had a message, just before I came here, from Gabrielle Carnet. She found a hundred thousand guilders, which must be the sum of your twenty thousand and the eighty thousand Mrs. Carnet collected from her company's bank account recently. Do you have any idea what she may have wanted to do with that eighty thousand?"

"No."

"The hundred thousand was found under her mattress,

a strange hiding place, don't you think? She did have a safe."

The baboon's hand reached out to a side table and came back with a pack of cigarettes. He smiled apologetically. "Time to smoke. Under the mattress, you said, that *is* a strange place. I know her safe. It isn't really a safe: it's fireproof but not burglarproof, it opens with a normal key. She never kept much money in there. I made a hiding place in her bedroom, under a loose board. It has a spring lock. You have to press a very small knob near one of the legs of her bed. If she wanted to hide money she would have hidden it in there."

Nothing was said for a while and the commissaris looked around. The apartment seemed to consist of only one room stretching from the front to the rear of the house. The furniture was sparse but of good quality, not from the showrooms of Carnet and Company. Good Victorian furniture and not too much of it. A quiet room, refined, with large empty surfaces, both in floor and wall space. The sergeant had got up and was wandering around.

"Sir?"

The commissaris got up too. The sergeant was looking at a painting. The painting showed a rat realistically drawn, each long brittle hair in place, the mouth half open showing pointed cruel teeth, the red eye glared. It was rearing on its spindly hind legs and its long tail, of an obscene, glaring naked pink, hung down.

"Unusual, don't you think, sir?"

The tail went beyond the painting, curving over its frame and continuing on the wall. The part that protruded from the painting's flat surface had become three-dimensional, molded out of some plastic material but so well shaped that it seemed alive. There was another strange detail in the painter's subject matter. The rat was ridden by a little boy dressed in a dainty suit of dark red velvet.

The childish face sat in a high collar of ruffled lace, and the boy's small pudgy hands held reins that were slipped through the rat's mouth.

"Do you like it?" the baboon's voice asked from the

other side of the room.

"It wasn't made to be liked, I think." The commissaris was still studying the painting. "Your work, Mr. Vleuten?"

"In a way. The combination is mine. The original is an illustration to a child's tale and I enlarged it and worked in some of the details. I've done more work like this, more elaborate, but in the same vein, I would think."

The baboon got up and pressed a button at the side of a large cupboard. A deep hum filled the room and the cupboard's door swung open. The apparition that rode out of the cupboard came straight at the sergeant, who jumped out of its way, but it changed direction and he had to jump again. The commissaris wasn't able to determine the nature of the apparition immediately, he only knew he felt nauseated.

He followed it as it moved around and returned to the cupboard.

It was a structure of human bones, clipped together and held upright by a transparent plastic rod. The head seemed to be a cow's skull, very old and moldy, with a gaping hole in its forehead framed in dry moss. Part of the skull was covered by a mask of frayed purple corduroy but the eye sockets and the long mouth with rows of pale yellow teeth had been left bare. The cupboard's door closed and the hum stopped. The commissaris looked at the floor. A pair of rails had been sunk into the smooth polished boards, evidently the specter had ridden on a small cart powered by electricity.

"A toy," the baboon said.

De Gier was staring at the cupboard door, his legs astride. Grijpstra stood next to the sergeant, bent slightly forward. Only the commissaris hadn't moved, not even when the ghoul's weapon, a rusted Sten gun, had brushed the back of his sleeve.

He sat down again. "You are an artist, Mr. Vleuten, and your creations are spectacular. I'm sure the municipal museum would be interested and give you space to exhibit. I'm interested too. What prompted you to make that structure?''

"A vision," the baboon said slowly, "a vision when I was drunk. I don't normally drink much, but I did happen to get very drunk some years ago and I passed out. My body stopped functioning but my mind worked well, too well, perhaps. The sensation was unpleasant. I wanted to go to sleep but I had been caught in a maelstrom. You probably know the experience. Dizziness, increasing until everything turns, not only what the mind experiences but the mind itself joins its reflections. A crazy dance, and in my case also macabre.''

The commissaris smiled. "If I remember correctly that particular sensation doesn't last too long. One gets sick and vomits and then there is nothing but sleep until the hangover the following day.''

"I didn't get sick. I spent hours being part of the maelstrom, trying not to be sucked into the abyss that lurked at its bottom. I had everything against me that night. There was much to be seen although I didn't want to see it. In the edge of the swirl different scenes were acted out and I was in all of them. The main actors, apart from myself, were a human skeleton with a masked cow's head and a little boy riding his rat.''

It was the commissaris's turn to get up and wander around the room and the baboon followed him. They were of about the same height and Grijpstra leaned out of his chair to keep track of their moving shapes.

"So what have we caught now?" de Gier whispered.

"Shhh!''

"Normally a man would try to get away from his fears," the commissaris was saying, "but you went to great trouble to picture them. It seems that you do the opposite of what is to be expected. The effort is deliberate?''

"Yes.''

"Like when you had the Carnet and Company firm in the palm of your hand, so to speak, and you threw it away?''

"Yes.''

"Would you mind a personal question?''

"No."

"Patient, isn't he?" de Gier's voice said close to Grijpstra's ear. Grijpstra's hands made an irritated flapping movement in response.

"You have a nickname, Mr. Vleuten. You are called the baboon. It would seem to me that you wouldn't like that nickname. A baboon is an ape. I would have expected pictures of baboons in this room, maybe even skeletons of baboons."

The baboon laughed. "I have several mirrors here, I can see the baboon anytime I wish to and often when I don't wish to." The laugh was relaxed and spread to the three detectives.

"True. Another question, something that interests me, it has nothing to do with why we are here. Your effort is to do the opposite of what is expected and your effort must require strength. It is easier to glide along the groove. You are exerting yourself to go against that movement, to break out of the groove altogether, perhaps. Does that effort get you anywhere?"

The baboon had come back to his chair and sat down. His flat strong hands rested on his knees. "An intriguing question."

"Yes. Would you answer it?"

"Why not? But I don't think I can. Perhaps the vision I tried to describe just now set me off. Everything was going so well at that time, you see. I was, in a way, making a career. I was selling unbelievable quantities of furniture. My income was based, in part, on commission, so I was earning a fair amount of money. On top of that I could have the business, the control of it, anyway. Bergen had weakened to the point where he was ready to have himself pushed out. Elaine wanted to marry me and it wouldn't have been an impossible match, we are of the same age and I was fond of her. But nothing was happening."

"How do you mean, Mr. Vleuten?"

"I was just driving a car, visiting customers, going home in the evenings, resting during the weekends. I had a boat, of course, and there were other pastimes, hobbies. I read,

I painted a little. But still nothing was happening. I just moved along.''

"And you were bored?"

"No. I became bored after that drunken night. It seemed there was something else. But whatever that something else was, it was certainly frightening. The rat and the little boy, the skeleton threatening me. I don't know whether you felt threatened just now, as it lunged at you from the cupboard. Perhaps to you it was just a silly shape like something you see at a carnival, something you scream at and then forget again. To me the shapes were much more, they came out of my own mind, out of the hidden part of my mind, and they were very strong. I was frightened throughout the vision, but I was also fascinated even while I was being tortured by the little boy—he isn't as harmless as he looks, you know—and chased by his rat and even as the cow shape attacked me over and over again, hurting me badly every time. And it wasn't just masochism. I don't particularly enjoy being in pain, but yet . . .''

"You decided consciously to live with your fear? To deliberately recreate it?"

"I decided to try that. I'm not original. I'm quite content to follow ways already explored. I assume that you are acquainted with the work of Bosch, Breughel. There have been others, also now, the films of Fellini, for instance. And there are writers, poets, even composers . . .''

"Many who follow those paths go mad, Mr. Vleuten. They commit suicide, are found hanging in alleys, afloat in the canals, lifeless in gutters. We find them, our patrol cars bring them in and dump them in the morgue.''

The baboon's chest expanded as he breathed. "No, the corpses you find have a different history. Drug addicts and alcoholics are caught in a groove too, they slip into habits like average citizens. I want to do something else, really *do* something, not to slip into a ready-made pattern that has, at the best, some moments of high perception but leads to utter degeneration eventually. The idea is not so bad perhaps; it's romantic to be a tramp, I thought of that possibility. I even spent some time in Paris studying clochards, but I decided that their way of life is both uncomfortable and unnecessary and leads to what most lives lead to, a half-conscious dream that turns in a half-circle. The clochards I followed around had to beg or steal. I didn't want to do that, even though the idea of being nothing, having nothing, not even a name, did appeal to me. But I wouldn't want to break into some tourist's car to be able to buy my next bottle or teaspoon of drugs. Why should I spoil another man's vacation? The tourist has his rights too. I don't quarrel with the ideals or lack of ideals of others. But it was interesting to live with the clochards for a while. Some of them were as sinister, as horrible, as my vision, but it seemed that I could prick through them. They were shadows, my vision was more real.''

"The clochards weren't getting anywhere, you mean?''

"Oh, they were somewhere all right, in hell. A hell of boredom, not so different from my own when I was selling a lot of furniture.''

"And now, are you bored now?''

"No.''

"Happy?''

The baboon shook his head. "Happy! That's a silly word. It has to do with security, there *is* no security. The only thing we can ever be secure about is the knowledge that we will die.''

"Do you feel that you are getting anywhere?''

"No, but perhaps I am approaching . . .''

"Approaching what?''

The sergeant was listening with such concentration that his eyes had become slits. The conversation, intense, almost ominous in its inward direction, sounded familiar. He could understand both the significance of the questions and the penetration of the answers. It seemed, and the possibility didn't appear so ludicrous later when he thought back on it, that the meeting between baboon and commissaris was staged for his own personal benefit. There was an accord between the old man and the bizarre figure opposite him that didn't have to be stressed, they would have understood each other without the question-and-answer game.

But some of de Gier's own thoughts were being clarified in a way that made the game seem staged.

He glanced at Grijpstra, but the adjutant's initial fascination had ebbed away. De Gier knew that Grijpstra had gone back to his task, the apprehension of Elaine Carnet's killer. He guessed, and the guess was substantiated later when he talked about the investigation again, that Grijpstra thought that the commissaris was only interested in determining the suspect's character, to see if he could be fitted into the facts they had collected about Elaine's death. No more, no less. The ideal policeman.

"A mystery perhaps." The baboon's answer had a mocking overtone. His hand, each finger moving individually, mocked the answer.

"Yes, a mystery," the commissaris said pleasantly. "A useless word, I agree. Well, sir, we'll be going. Just a last question about Mrs. Carnet's death. Could you think of anyone who would derive some pleasure, some gain, from her death? There are a number of suspects we are interrogating. There is Mr. Bergen, young Mr. Pullini, Gabrielle too, of course. There may be others, people Mrs. Carnet employed, perhaps. We found a man, a certain Mr. de Bree, a neighbor, who tried to poison Gabrielle Carnet's dog some days ago."

The baboon didn't answer.

"You have no ideas that could be of help to us?"

"Only negative ideas. Mr. Bergen is mainly a businessman. He was, when I knew him, quite happy to run the business, I don't think he wanted to own it. And with Elaine's death he will still only own a quarter of the shares, the quarter she gave him years ago, the other three-quarters will go to Gabrielle. Did you mention Pullini?"

"Yes, Francesco Pullini. He is in town just now. We saw him briefly today, he isn't feeling well."

"I know Francesco. He dealt with Bergen, not with Elaine."

The commissaris sat up and massaged his thighs.

"Is that so? I understand that Mrs. Carnet did pay attention to the Pullini connection, chose merchandise, determined the size of the orders, and so on."

The baboon shook his head. "Not really, that was just a charade. Bergen liked to work on Francesco and he sometimes got Elaine to help. Tricks: he would give a very large order to get a good price and then he would later halve it and say that Elaine had made the decision, or he might delay the order altogether, also to get a better price."

"And Gabrielle, she didn't get on too well with her mother, I believe?"

"True, they did argue sometimes, but Gabrielle has had her own apartment for quite a long time now."

"Whose idea was that?"

"Gabrielle's. She is clever, and she certainly loved her mother. She could have moved out altogether but she stayed in the house."

"Did Mrs. Carnet drink compulsively?"

The baboon moved a hand over his face. "Yes, I think so, the drinking was getting worse. Couldn't she have fallen down the stairs?"

The commissaris got up. "Yes, she might have, that would certainly be the best solution."

"Where's your car?" the commissaris asked when they were in the street again.

"A little farther along, sir, near the Berlaghe Bridge."

"I'll give you a ride. Sergeant?"

"Sir."

"I know it's been a long day but I'd like you to go back to the Pulitzer Hotel and get Francesco's passport. If he doesn't want to give it up you can bring him to headquarters and lock him in for the night. I'll clear it with the public prosecutor later on, but if you are tactful that won't be necessary. Grijpstra?"

"Sir."

"Do you want to go home now?"

"Not particularly, sir."

"You can come with me, I want to pay another call on Mr. Bergen. You haven't met him yet."

He opened the door of the Citroën and took out the radio's microphone.

"Headquarters?"

"Headquarters, who is calling?"

"CID, the Carnet case. Any news from Detective Cardozo?"

"Yes, sir, he left a number, wants you to call him."

"Any urgency?"

"No, sir."

He pushed the microphone back. "I'll call him from Bergen's house."

"We might have dinner somewhere, sir," Grijpstra said from the back of the car.

"Later, if you don't mind. I'd like to see Bergen first. Would you like to have dinner with us, sergeant?"

"Thank you, sir, but I'll have to go home first to feed Tabriz and I'd like to get out of this uniform and have a shower."

"Fine, how about nine o'clock at that Chinese restaurant next to the porno cinema in the old city? We've eaten there before, it's a favorite hangout of yours, I believe."

"Cardozo might like to come too, sir. He's been complaining that he is always sent off on his own and that he loses track of what goes on."

The commissaris smiled. "Yes, and he is right, of course. But I have his number and I'll ring him later. He's probably having his dinner now but he can have it again. By nine o'clock our preliminary investigation should be complete. It'll be time to compare our theories, if we have the courage to bring them out, and to move into the next stage."

"Setting up traps, sir?"

The commissaris turned around. "No, Grijpstra, the traps have been set up already and not by us. This time we'll have to do the opposite, if we can. We'll have to release our suspects, they are trapped already."

"The opposite," de Gier murmured. "Interesting."

12

Cardozo marched along, arms swinging, until he became aware of his own eagerness and dropped back into an exaggerated slouch. He had been out of uniform for some two years now, but he hadn't yet lost the habit of being on patrol during working hours. He was still checking bicycles for proper lights and would start every time he saw a car going through the red. He also missed the protection of his mate. Policemen on the beat are hardly ever alone, detectives often are. His trained eyes were registering.

The neighborhood wasn't known for crime but there were still traces. A young man on the other side of the street was moving about hazily. Drugs? Or just tiredness after a long day at grammar school? A badly dressed foreigner, possibly a Turk, a man with a wide brown face and a heavy coal black mustache, seemed interested in a bicycle thrown against a fence. A thief? Or an unskilled laborer on his way to an overcrowded room in a cheap boarding house in the next quarter, which was only a mile from there. Cardozo shrugged, he shouldn't bother the man, even if he stole a bicycle right in front of his eyes. He was a murder brigade detective, a specialist. But he crossed the street. The Turk had stopped and was bending down to examine the bicycle's lock. Cardozo's hand touched the man's shoulder. He shook his head and pulled back his jacket so that the pistol's butt shone against his white shirt.

"Police. Move along now."

The man's teeth showed in a lopsided grin of fear. "Only looking."

"Sure. Move along."

The man stepped aside and began to run. Cardozo noted the man's shoes, the soles had worn through. The seat of the man's trousers was patched, badly, with a piece of different cloth. Poverty, a rare occurrence in Amsterdam, but the Turk would be outside the cradle of social security. If he starved he starved, there would be nowhere to go. Cardozo had only been introduced to poverty once, when he was on his way back from France during a holiday and had lost his wallet with his money and train ticket, slipped through a tear in his unlined summer jacket. He had noticed the wallet's absence in a restaurant, just before he had begun to read the menu, and had wandered out into the street again. Lunchtime without lunch, in Paris where he didn't know the way and could hardly ask for directions for lack of words. It had taken him all day to walk out of the city and find the expressway, and he had waited for hours at the side of the road as night fell and the traffic's flow began to show gaps, long black lulls that increased as the night crept on. He had drunk from a tap at a gas station, suspiciously eyed by attendants in crisp uniforms. No coffee, no cigarettes. He had bummed a cigarette from another hitchhiker and smoked it hungrily. The hitchhiker was professional, a tanned young man carrying a brand-new shoulder pack stuck on aluminium tubes. A sporting type with muscular legs and high boots and an insulated windbreaker and an American flag sewed on his pack. An efficient traveler who had planned his trip through Europe and who had his money in traveler's checks, folded in a clip and buttoned away in his breast pocket. Cardozo had been carrying an old suitcase, reinforced with a frayed belt, and had shivered in the early morning's chill, a lost little figure who was refused, with an imperative wave of her bejeweled and manicured hand, by the lady who gave the American his lift. Cardozo remembered the loneliness and hunger of the two days he had needed to get home, and the memory showed later when he had to deal with the lost and strayed of his own city.

The Turk disappeared around the corner and Cardozo followed slowly, turning again into the Mierisstraat. He pulled the polished bell handle and waited patiently until he heard Gabrielle's voice behind the heavy oak door that swung open slowly, screening her.

"I'm sorry, I was just about to take a shower when you rang. I saw you through my window."

"It's all right, miss, I've come to ask you about that money you found. We heard about your telephone call through the radio but there were no details."

"Come in, come in, we can talk inside."

She was going up the stairs as he pushed his way through the glass door of the hall. Her bare feet were tripping out of sight at the staircase's curve, they hardly seemed to touch the thick rug. The housecoat had fallen open when she welcomed him in the hall. He had seen the outline of her body as she hastily retied the sash. A small body, the body of a very young girl but with the fully developed breasts of a woman. She had said she was nearly thirty years old.

The terrier was waiting for them in Gabrielle's sitting room. He greeted the visitor and Cardozo bent down and scratched the dog's head and rubbed the firm woolly ears.

"Has he recovered now?"

She laughed. "Yes, completely. We've been for a walk this afternoon, I don't dare to let him out in the garden. Are you still working on Paul's case? Or isn't it important anymore?"

"Yes, miss. We know who gave him the arsenic."

"Who?" Gabrielle's voice had lost its purr and the green eyes were drilling into Cardozo's face.

"I can't tell you yet, miss, not until a summons has been issued, but that won't be long now. I expect that the poisoner will have to go to court. The judge has been rather fierce on cases of this sort lately. Our man will probably have to pay a fine and damages to you, and there may be a suspended jail sentence of a few weeks."

"Good. I think I know who it is. That horrible cat was in the garden again this afternoon. I threw a rock at it but I missed. I can't stand that cat with its two faces. It was the cat's owner, right? Mr. de Bree?"

Cardozo shook his head. "I can't tell you yet, miss, but you will be informed in due time. We have a confession, you see, but a confession on its own means nothing. People have been known to admit all sorts of criminal deeds that they had nothing to do with. The public prosecutor will have to evaluate the case but I think it is pretty clear. We also have statements signed by witnesses."

"Good." Her hand came up shyly and touched his hair. "I'm glad you're with the police, I trusted you from the first time I saw you. How is the investigation about my mother going?"

"We are working."

"Can I get you a drink?"

Cardozo looked at his watch. "Perhaps not, miss. I am still on duty."

"Oh, nonsense, it's after hours now. I'll have a drink with you, and please call me Gabrielle. We don't have to be so formal, this is the third time we've met. Whiskey?"

"You don't have vodka, Gabrielle?"

She giggled. "Vodka doesn't smell, they say. Do you still have to report today?"

He nodded. The gauze undercurtains of the room were drawn and the light was soft and restful. He felt tired and the low couch lured him to lean back and forget. He saw the girl open a cupboard and heard a bottle's gurgle. She left for a moment and came back with a pitcher filled with ice cubes.

Cardozo's lips split in a happy sensuous smirk. This was the true police life, the adventurous scene he had so often dreamed himself into at the movies and in the short but vivid imaginations pressed into pauses between his alarm clock's piercing shrieks. The weary detective enjoying a break. The room was just right. His gaze rested briefly on some delicately arranged flowers, on the rows of books, on the soft orange and brown border of the Oriental carpet covering most of the floor. Gabrielle gave him a glass. The drink was properly prepared with a slice of fresh lemon stuck on the side and the ice tinkling through a blurred mixture of vodka and club soda. He saw Gabrielle's breasts, only for a moment again, for the housecoat closed as she straightened up.

He also saw the small object between her breasts, the skull of a cow carved from a small piece of gleaming walnut. A beautifully chiseled miniature with deep eye sockets and a protruding mouth, each tiny jaw complete with its teeth. Between the minute horns the forehead showed a cavity, perhaps a natural fault of the wood, forming an extra eye and accentuating the skull's ghoulish threat.

She had squatted down at his feet and her eyes sparkled in the semidarkness. A small wave of guilt prompted his question.

"You found some money, I was told. A lot of money? How did that come about?"

"I was cleaning my mother's bedroom and stripping her bed. The bills were under the mattress, stuck in a magazine. You want to see them?"

"Please."

He sat up while she was away. A small painting caught his eye. It was hung in a dark corner near the end of the couch and he bent over to study it closer. A portrait of a young man, head and shoulders. A young man in some medieval costume, a tight tunic that fitted the narrow shoulders closely. A striking face framed in long, dark, flowing hair. A hooked nose, large liquid eyes, a high forehead. A nobleman from the South, Italian, Spanish, perhaps a Spanish don from the time that Spain was trying to conquer the Netherlands. He wondered what had moved Gabrielle to hang the portrait in the intimacy of her room, so close to her bed. Whenever she lay on her right side the young man would be staring at her. He heard her in the corridor and moved to the middle of the couch. She came back with a ladies' magazine and opened it and they counted the notes together, one hundred notes of a thousand guilders each. Eighty were brand-new, twenty slightly used.

"I don't suppose I should keep the money here. Do you need it as an exhibit? You could give me a receipt; I suppose the police would return it later?"

The small hand on his wrist distracted him but he could still think logically. "No. Just hide it until tomorrow and deposit it in your bank account. I have seen the money and I'll make up a report and sign it under oath."

Her purring voice laughed. "Yes, you are an official, a police officer. I can't believe it. You must be very dangerous, nobody would ever expect you to be a detective. How clever of the police to employ you. I am sure people will tell you anything you want to know!"

"You mean I look like a harmless moron?"

Her hand was stroking his neck. "Never mind, I am only teasing. I like you very much. I like men who don't look tall and overpowering and handsome like that other officer who came the night of Mother's death, the beautiful man with the large mustache. Men like that are unbearable."

Cardozo was nodding and smiling, but the little wave of guilt had crept back and he heard himself defending the sergeant. "But he is very good, I have worked with him for a long time now. He is very intelligent and dependable."

"Pff. He is a showoff!" She looked at her watch. "Oh, for heaven's sake. I *must* take my shower. It was such a hot day and I'll have to go work again. If I don't bathe I'll be prickly and irritable and nothing will go right. I promised Mr. Bergen that I would sort out his stock files. We are preparing a statement of what we have in our warehouse for the bank, and so far we come up with a different figure every time. I'll have to check through the invoices again."

She jumped up but held on to his wrist so that he was pulled off the couch. He was in the bathroom before he knew that she had taken him with her and he saw her drop her housecoat and step into the tub and adjust the faucets. He stood, holding his glass, trying to find a harmless object to look at. She laughed. "Silly! Haven't you ever seen a naked woman? Why don't you sit on the toilet and enjoy your drink. I'll be ready in a moment."

The shower came on. The bath had plastic curtains but

she didn't draw them. He saw the hot water splash on her shoulders and run down her arms and there was a small riverlet trickling between her breasts, with two sidelines running down and causing a steady drip from her nipples.

"Don't you want to see me like this?"

But he did want to, of course, and he was having trouble with his breathing. He took her by the hand before she had had a chance to reach for the towel.

"But I'm still wet."

He pulled the towel off the rack and wrapped it around her body and swept her off her feet and carried her through the corridor. Her head rested on his shoulder.

On the bed he saw the arrogant eyes of the Spanish nobleman and he pushed the portrait's broad gold frame so that it slid off its hook and got stuck between the couch and the wall. The terrier was watching too, its dark button eyes fixed on the linked, throbbing bodies. The dog's fuzzy ears stood up, quivering with interest, and his short tail tapped on the side of his basket. Cardozo wasn't aware that some of his passion was shared by Paul, and when, after a while, he turned over and looked at the room, the dog had curled himself up in a tight ball and was fast asleep.

13

The Citroën's smooth shape was coasting through the avenues of Amsterdam Old South like a large predator fish patrolling its hunting streams. It had been cruising for twenty-five minutes and it kept on turning the same corners. Grijpstra was studying a small soiled map and gave directions that the commissaris found hard to follow. Every turnoff they tried led into one-way streets and they invariably tried to enter on the wrong side. If Grijpstra had been with de Gier his mood might have turned sour and been edging toward blind fury, but the commissaris's presence had soothed his mind and he continued trying to trace a course while the car floated on.

"It can't be here anyway," the commissaris said quietly. "Look at those vast houses, they were patricians' homes once. Homes for the aged now, adjutant, and private hospitals and maybe a few high-priced sex clubs tucked away here and there. The whole neighborhood is subsidized by the state now." He smiled. "Or lust, and expense accounts that cater to lust. Lovely old places all the same, don't you agree?"

Grijpstra looked up from the map. The heavily wooded gardens lining the curving avenue did indeed offer a spectacle of sedate grandeur. The gardens shielded four- and five-storied villas, decorated with turrets and cantilevered balconies overgrown with creepers, abodes of splendor where merchants had once planned their overseas adventures and enjoyed the benefits of constructive but greedy thoughts.

"Yes, sir. But we should be close, we have been close for a while now. The street behind this one must be the one we want, I'm sure of it. Some mansions were pulled down and a bungalow park has taken their sites. Bergen probably has one of the bungalows, but I wouldn't know how to get in there with all these damned NO ENTRY signs."

The commissaris tried again. "No. No use. We'll walk."

They heard the evening song of a thrush the minute the engine was shut off and the commissaris pointed at the bird, a small, exact silhouette on an overhead wire. The thrush flew off and a nightingale took over. Grijpstra had folded his map and put it away and began to walk on, but the commissaris restrained him, waiting for the end of the trilling cantata. The nightingale seemed to feel that he had an audience, for he pushed himself into such a brilliant feat of pure artistry, and sang so loudly, that Grijpstra expected him to fall off his branch. When the song broke, and ended, in the middle of a rapidly rising scale of notes, the commissaris was standing on his toes, his small head raised, his eyes closed.

Grijpstra smiled. It was good to be with the old man again. His perception had risen and he became aware of the quiet of the street. The one-way system had effectively blocked all through traffic and the old-fashioned streetlights, adapted gas lanterns spaced far apart, threw a soft light that was held by flowering bushes and freshly mowed lawns and hung between the gnarled branches of old beeches and oaks. They walked on, two contemplative pedestrians enjoying the peace of the evening, and found Bergen's street at the next corner.

Grijpstra checked the house numbers. "This one, sir."

The bungalow's garage doors were open. A new Volvo had been left in the driveway, unable to fit into the garage, where the wreck of a small, fairly new car blocked its way. The compact's nose had been pushed in and its hood stood up, cracked. A refrigerator with its door hanging open leaned against the wreck and parts of a lawn mower littered the floor.

"I'm sure most of that could be fixed," Grijpstra said as he peered into the garage. The commissaris had walked on. "Maybe that's considered to be junk, adjutant, the throwouts of a different lifestyle."

The commissaris pushed the bell. The door swung open and Bergen was staring at them, one eye large and round and menacing, the other almost closed. He was holding his face and his spectacles hung on one ear. He was in his shirtsleeves and his suspenders were slipping off his shoulders.

"Do you mind if we come in, Mr. Bergen? We're sorry having to disturb you again today, but we won't be long."

Bergen stepped back and they walked through a hall, stumbling over a pair of rubber boots and two or three coats dropped on the floor, and stopped in the corridor. The door to the kitchen was ajar, and Grijpstra saw a heap of dirty dishes dumped into the sink. There was a smell of burned meat. Bergen passed them and opened the door to the living room. He was still holding his cheek. His voice sounded muffled and, after he dropped his hand, slurred. Grijpstra sniffed; there was no smell of alcohol.

Bergen shifted a pile of laundry on the settee and motioned for the commissaris to sit down. Grijpstra had found a leather recliner, next to a waste basket overflowing with crumpled newspapers topped by banana peels.

"Your wife isn't back yet, Mr. Bergen?"

Bergen had found a chair too and faced the commissaris dumbly.

The commissaris asked the question again.

"No. It's a mess here. I've been camping out, more or less, waiting for her to come back. She won't. There was a letter in the mail today, a lawyer's letter. She wants a divorce."

"I'm sorry to hear that."

Bergen muttered something.

"Pardon?"

"Can't speak so well, paralysis, you know." The word "paralysis" seemed to be causing him considerable trouble.

"It's all right, sir, we can understand you. I must really apologize for this intrusion, but we're still working on Mrs. Carnet's death, as you will understand."

Bergen's round eye stared fiercely. "Any progress, commissaris?"

"Some, we hope. But what's this about your face? Your office told us that you had some tests done this afternoon. The results are encouraging, I hope?"

"No."

"Oh, dear."

"No. Terrible day. This started last night but I didn't think it was anything serious until this morning, and when I got to the hospital they told me they were busy and wouldn't have time for me for a few days. I found a private clinic and the specialist said that I needed a skull photograph, an X-ray. Here." He got up and rummaged through a stack of papers on a side table, impatiently tossing the top sheets on the ground. "Here. This isn't the photograph but a report that has to do with it. They found a spot, a white spot, chalk, and they said there might be something behind it that they couldn't see. Read it for yourself."

The commissaris took the sheet and put on his glasses. He began to mumble his way through the photocopy's faint print. "Hmm. Technical talk. Let's see. *The chloroid plexuses are calcified bilaterally, left greater than right. There is a small area of calcification that appears to be in contact with the right frontal calvarium and measured to be greater than one hundred seventy-five EMI density units.* Hm hm. And here we seem to have some sort of conclusion. *In spite of this, the presence of a small underlying meningioma cannot be ruled out entirely.*"

He peered at Bergen over his glasses. "Is that so bad, Mr. Bergen? I'm afraid I don't understand the terminology. It would just seem that they found a little chalk somewhere in your skull. What's a meningioma?"

Bergen's reply was unclear and he repeated it. "A tumor, and a tumor would mean cancer, brain cancer."

The commissaris read on. " *'Further serial studies sug-gested.'* " He gave the paper back and sat down. "Yes. So what they are saying is that the chalk *could* hide a tumor, and then perhaps we might assume that the tumor *could* indicate cancer. But there is no need to jump to conclusions. Were these further serial tests in fact done?"

"Not all of them. I'll have to go again tomorrow and the neurologist said he would know then. I took this copy with me and showed it to my doctor but he wouldn't say anything. They never do when they suspect cancer."

"I see."

The silence lasted for a while, and Bergen's eye, the lid drawn away by the paralyzed nerve, kept on boring into the commissaris's face.

"This really is not the time to disturb you, Mr. Bergen, and I'm sorry about coming here, but what can we do? You heard that Gabrielle located a hundred thousand guilders under her mother's mattress?"

"Won't do any good," Bergen muttered. "She said she would pay it back into the company's account. Eighty thousand; the rest she'll keep, of course, that's Elaine's private money. But on top of everything else I had this letter delivered by messenger. A letter from the bank."

He jumped up and began to look through the papers on the side table again. "You know what this is?"

"No idea, Mr. Bergen."

"A note to say that the bank is curtailing the company's credit. For a few years now the bank has let us borrow a million, and we have been using that credit, of course, and now they have decided to cut that in half. Any money paid in by us from now on will be taken out of our account until we have paid in half a million. They *would* send the letter today. With Elaine dead they're worried about their pennies."

The commissaris sat up and pushed his glasses back. "Really? They have no faith in your presidency of the company?"

"So it seems." Bergen had dropped the letter on the floor. "The manager has come to see Elaine and me a couple of times this year. He had noticed that we were using our full credit continuously and he wasn't impressed by my last balance sheet. I have been selling large quantities at minimal profit and we have a lot of stock. I told him it was all right. I'm aiming for government business and the transactions are profitable, so why should he be anxious?"

"But he is, evidently."

"An idiot." Bergen's mouth curved on one side. "A perfect idiot. He even suggested that we should hire the baboon again. I think he is a personal friend of Vleuten's. He sort of suggested that we shouldn't have fired the baboon and I told him that we never did, that the man left by his own free will, that he resigned."

"The profit margin of your business was better when Mr. Vleuten was still on your staff?"

"Yes, but since then we have had more competition. Business always has its ups and downs. I am trying to get better prices from Pullini now and we have a new salesman on the road. The pendulum will swing back again. But it's hard to convince a bank manager, and with Elaine's death . . ."

"I see, a new factor to be considered or, rather, the lack of an old factor. Gabrielle will replace her mother, I imagine?"

"The bank is not impressed by Gabrielle."

The commissaris sighed. "I see you have some problems, sir, but problems can be overcome. I'm sure you'll find a way. Just one question before we go. Do you have any idea why Mrs. Carnet took out that eighty thousand on the day of her death?"

Bergen's hands moved about on his skull. The silvery hair that had been so stately during their interview of the morning stood up in tufts. "No."

"Carnet and Company owe that amount to Pullini, isn't that so?"

"Yes, but that had nothing to do with Elaine. She left the day-to-day management to me, she never interfered anymore. She did read our list of creditors every month and she may have known that eighty thousand was payable to

Pullini, but why would she concern herself with that? And even if she did intend to pay that debt, why would she pay it in cash? She could have given Pullini a check and he would have cashed the check himself. We don't like to move banknotes around, nobody does."

Grijpstra had gotten up and was looking out through the garden doors. An untidy collection of clumsily sawed logs was pushed against the low stone wall of the terrace. There were scattered and broken roof tiles on the terrace and red stains of crumbled bricks, knocked out by the tree's falling trunk. He walked back to the center of the room and looked at Bergen's trousers and hands. No, they were clean. Bergen hadn't touched his tree today. But even so, the alibi was thin. The tree wouldn't have taken all evening. He could have used his Volvo to visit Mrs. Carnet, a few minutes' ride.

"Have you seen everybody now?" Bergen asked.

"I think so. We saw your friend Mr. Vleuten this afternoon."

Bergen's hand waved tiredly. "Not my friend. Perhaps the baboon was right to get out of the business. He's doing very well, isn't he?"

"I thought you had had no contact with him since he left. That was awhile ago, wasn't it?"

"I heard," Bergen said. "We have mutual acquaintances. The baboon is doing well. He restored his house, he deals in boats. Boats are the thing these days, everybody who does well wants one. Old boats, antique launches, flat-bottomed sailing yachts . . . excellent status symbols. The baboon is a businessman still, he hasn't forgotten what he learned when he was selling our furniture. And Elaine must have been providing him with capital, she has been saving her wages and profits for the last five years. She used to put them back into the business but stopped when we obtained good bank credit. And she always loved Vleuten. The baboon is the clever one and I am the sucker. I work and he plays around."

"Well, that's one way of looking at it, no doubt there are other ways. But we did see Mr. Vleuten and we also talked with Mr. Pullini.''

Bergen laughed cheerlessly and his hand came up to hold his cheek again. ''Pullini!''

''You don't think there's a connection?''

''No, Francesco hardly knew Elaine. His father did business with her and she went to Italy, but that was all such a long time ago. She was still working then.''

''We'll have to be on our way again, Mr. Bergen. I wish you good luck with your test tomorrow.''

''Poor man,'' Grijpstra said in the car.

''You think so, adjutant?''

Grijpstra's right eyebrow crept up an eighth of an inch. ''Shouldn't I be sorry for the slob, sure? He is in about as perfect a mess as Job on his garbage pile. Bergen has lost it all, hasn't he?''

The commissaris suddenly tittered and Grijpstra's eyebrow stayed where it was. ''An absolute fool, adjutant. The man must have a special talent for connecting misunderstandings incorrectly. That medical report didn't indicate cancer, it only said there might be something somewhere. Doctors like to be explorers, especially when they have a lot of expensive equipment around that can be used in their explorations. All they have to do is instill a little fear in the patient's mind and they can switch on their electronic gear and work up a bill of a few thousand guilders. And the insurance pays.''

''But there could be a tumor in Bergen's head, sir.''

The commissaris shrugged. ''Surely, and in my head and in yours, but we haven't thought of that possibility yet. Bergen has.''

''So you don't think there is any link between his paralysis and whatever they are looking for in his head?''

''Not necessarily. What Bergen has now I've had too, Bell's palsy, a harmless affliction that will go away by itself. I didn't want to tell Bergen that. I'm not a doctor and perhaps he *is* in serious trouble. I'm only saying that the man is overworrying, about everything.''

''His divorce and the bank letter?''

''Exactly. Calamities are only calamities if you define

them as such; in reality there are only events and all events can be useful."

Grijpstra's eyebrow came down.

"You should know that simple truth," the commissaris continued. "You've been in the police a long time now, adjutant. We always deal with people, suspects or victims, who have managed to channel their thoughts in such a way that they see no acceptable way out anymore. They think they are suffering because of all sorts of reasons—their rights haven't been respected, they've lost something, they've been robbed or slandered or treated badly, and so they're justified in behaving in such a way that they break the law and meet us. But usually they are drowning in a poisonous pool of their own making. But they'll never blame themselves. Never."

The Citroën was waiting for a green light.

"Sir."

"Ah, thank you. No, Grijpstra, I won't pity our friend Bergen. Pity won't do any good, anyway. Let's hope he can get shocked out of his present state of mind and steer himself into a course that may lead to a little more freedom. And it's time to eat. And Cardozo wants to be telephoned. He must be brooding on the information he collected from his visit to Gabrielle."

The commissaris parked the car at the edge of the old city and, after calling Cardozo from a public telephone booth, they set out for the restaurant on foot. A brightly lit store window attracted the commissaris and he stopped to look in. He was still lecturing on the lack of awareness that causes illusion and misconstruction and didn't appear to notice what he was looking at.

Grijpstra cleared his throat.

"Yes, adjutant?"

Grijpstra pointed at the window. "I don't think this display is of much interest, sir."

The commissaris grinned and they walked on. The window had shown a number of different types of vibrators arranged on a ground of artificial grass that was fenced off by a row of plastic penises.

14

The fat god was grinning at the mongrel but the mongrel didn't care. She was lying on the floor of the cheap Chinese eating place, half hidden under a table, which everybody who knew the restaurant avoided because it wobbled, and was noisily licking her swollen private parts. She was a particularly ugly mongrel, small and hairy and spotted, but she did own some endearing features, such as large expressive eyes and a tail with a stiff curl that pointed at the spot where her neck should have been. De Gier's foot came out and nudged the dog. She looked up.

"Don't *do* that," de Gier whispered. "People are trying to eat here. The food is excellent but they won't taste it if you keep on making that blubbery sucking noise." The dog's tail quivered. She bared her teeth in an effort to be friendly and rolled over, showing her naked pink belly. De Gier's foot rubbed the belly softly and the dog whined ingratiatingly. The restaurant was empty and the owner, a tall thin Cantonese with the face of a philosopher, was resting his back against the counter; he hadn't moved in the last ten minutes.

The dog rolled back and went on licking and de Gier's eyes wandered up to the portrait of the fat god, a portly gentleman being crawled over by seven well-dressed slit-eyed toddlers equipped with similar smiles. The god of wealth and health, sitting on a cushion that in turn sat on a hilltop that overlooked a valley planted with dark green crops stretching to the horizon.

The restaurant's glass door swung open and Cardozo entered, followed by four street prostitutes coming in for a late dinner. Cardozo held the door and they thanked him politely. They were off duty now and had lost their inviting smiles and prancing mannerisms. De Gier knew them all: he had listened to them many times, he knew their favorite subjects. They never talked shop when they ate their fried rice or noodles. They liked to talk about knitting and the defects of their cars and about taxes, and they would linger over their meal, unwilling to go back to the street, where tourists, usually a little drunk, were ambling about restlessly, waiting to purchase their services.

"Evening," Cardozo said sadly.

De Gier muttered his reply and moved over to the corner chair so that Cardozo could sit next to him.

"Have you ordered?"

"No, I'm waiting for the commissaris, he should be here in a few minutes. We can have a beer."

He waved to the philosopher and put up two fingers. The Chinese bowed, pushed himself off the counter, and slid behind it, grabbing the handle of the beer pump before he had reached his proper station. His other hand swept two glasses off a shelf and caught them deftly; he had them in position as the first stream of frothy golden liquid poured out of the polished spout. The beer was on their table before de Gier's arm had come down.

"Your very good health. Had any adventures today?"

Cardozo nodded as he drank. "Yes, I saw Gabrielle Carnet just now. The commissaris wanted to know how she found the hundred thousand, you heard about that?"

"No. Tell me."

De Gier listened. "That's very nice, so the obvious motive has gone too, has it? What's this now, a complication or a simplification? I had worked out a theory but the facts may still fit. I'll have to talk to Grijpstra, maybe he thought

137

of the theory first, I forget now.''

Cardozo tried to smile. "Does it matter? You won't get any credit for it anyway. The case will be solved by the brigade and the chief constable will shake the commissaris's hand in the end or not. Maybe the public prosecutor will spoil the case, or the judge, or some fool lawyer.''

But de Gier hadn't heard him. The glass door swung open again and he was waving at the Chinese while the commissaris and Grijpstra came into the restaurant. Two more beers appeared and another ashtray.

"Sir?"

The commissaris had drunk his beer and was waiting for another. His hands moved restlessly on the bare boards of the table. "No, sergeant, Grijpstra can explain and then you three can fill each other in. I'll listen for a change.'' More beer appeared and the commissaris hid his face behind it.

Cardozo looked at Grijpstra, but the adjutant was reading the menu. "Roast pork, hmm. Fried noodles with shrimp, hmm. Wonton soup, that's nice but it's crossed out. Thin noodles with lobster, hmm, a little slippery but tasty. Yes.''

"Adjutant?"

"Yes. Noodles with fried chicken, I think, as always. I don't know why I bother to read the menu. And you'll have the same, de Gier, for otherwise we'll have to wait too long, and you'll have the same too, Cardozo. Sir?''

"I'll have the same.''

There was more beer again and then the food came and was eaten in silence. They listened to the prostitutes. The platinum blonde's little Fiat had lost its muffler and she had been given a ticket for causing excessive noise. The small redhead's Volkswagen had starting problems. The tall beauty with the German accent complained about a rattle in her Renault's front door. There didn't seem to be anything wrong with the black girl's car. De Gier was interested. He leaned over. "Excuse me, miss, what sort of a car do you drive?''

"A small Citroën.''

"Aha," the commissaris said.

"But it's brand-new, still under guarantee."

The commissaris turned around. "You won't have any trouble, miss. Citroëns are good cars, I've been driving them all my life. No trouble." The black girl smiled and the commissaris turned back to his fried noodles.

"No, sir?" Grijpstra whispered. "I thought you had a problem with your suspension a few weeks ago."

The commissaris's fork came up and pointed at the adjutant's face. "Minor. Little leak somewhere. They fixed it."

"And aren't they always fiddling around with the timing? The garage sergeant was telling me about that. He said it was driving him crazy."

"Nothing wrong with the timing, the sergeant wanted something to do."

"And . . ."

"Never mind. I think Cardozo wants to ask something, what is it, Cardozo?"

"I want to know everything, sir. I've only been working on the poisoned dog angle. I know nothing about the murder investigation. Who *are* our suspects, sir, and what have we found out?"

"Good. Adjutant, why don't you tell him, and then de Gier can do his bit too. And Cardozo can finish up. I haven't heard about Gabrielle Carnet and the hundred thousand guilders that popped up so conveniently. Go ahead, adjutant."

Grijpstra wanted more beer but was given coffee and the discussion started. It lasted for an hour as more coffee was consumed and Grijpstra's small black cigars smoldered away, making the restaurant's owner cough politely and turn on an electric fan.

"Do we know everything now?" the commissaris asked. "Yes, Cardozo?"

Cardozo seemed very ill at ease. His lips, holding the cigar that Grijpstra had forced on him, twisted spasmodically.

"Eh, sir, I would like to hear about that skeleton in the baboon's apartment again. It had a cow's skull, right?"

"Yes."

"Did, uh, the skull have a hole in its forehead?"

The commissaris thought. "Perhaps it did, yes. It was masked, a purple corduroy mask leaving the eye sockets open, but it seems that there was a sort of tear that exposed part of the forehead, a tear or a hole. Do you remember, sergeant?"

"Yes, sir. There was a hole in the skull's forehead, I remember it exactly, between the eyes but a little higher. The skull must have been very old, there was some dried-out crusted moss around that hole. But why do you ask, Cardozo?" His voice was honey sweet. "You weren't with us, Cardozo, so how do you know about that hole?"

"Uh . . ." Cardozo squeaked.

"Tell us, dear boy."

"Gabrielle was wearing a small object, on a nylon string," Cardozo said rapidly. "The object was a cow's skull, the size of, uh, like that." He pointed to a button on de Gier's denim jacket. "That size. It was carved out of walnut, I think, well done, a lot of detail. The eye sockets were quite deep and there was a third hole, I thought it was the fault of the wood."

"Amazing," de Gier said, still in the same sweet voice. "And how do you know that? I also saw a piece of nylon around the young lady's neck and I also saw a small object dangling on that nylon thread, but it was stuck way down into her blouse. I couldn't see any detail on that object and yet you describe it so accurately."

"I saw her this evening, before I came here. I told you, didn't I?"

"But how did you manage to see something she keeps between her breasts? She must have been naked. Why was she naked, dear boy? Did she strip, or did you forget your manners and rape the young lady?"

Grijpstra's eyes stared; the commissaris was stirring his coffee. Cardozo had picked up a match and was digging at a noodle, stuck between the table's boards.

"Maybe you should tell us what happened exactly," the commissaris said gently.

"I'm sorry, sir. I did have, uh, intimate contact with the suspect. I am very sorry, sir."

"She seduced you, did she?"

"No, sir, it was my own fault. I wasn't alert, I'm afraid. It, uh, just happened. I just slipped into it."

"Into what?" Grijpstra asked, frowning furiously.

"Gentlemen!" The commissaris said sternly and raised a forbidding hand. "Now, constable, you can give us some details. Try and describe exactly what happened. You can spare us the physical details, of course. She *did* seduce you, didn't she? I can't imagine that you instigated the action." The commissaris's voice was gentle again, he was stirring his coffee once more. Cardozo talked for a while.

"I see, well, never mind, Ah, I forgot to ask, did you see Francesco Pullini, de Gier? I want that passport." De Gier produced the passport and the commissaris opened it and looked at the photograph. "Good, was he upset?"

"Not particularly, sir, just a little, but Italians are rather excitable, I believe."

Cardozo picked up the passport and stared at the photograph. His eyes opened wide. "Sir!"

"What is it now, Cardozo? Don't tell me you know the man, you haven't met him."

"But I *do* know him, sir. There's a small portrait hanging behind the couch Gabrielle uses as a bed. An oil portrait. The face is very similar to this face, sir."

The commissaris breathed out slowly. His small wizened hand came out, reached across the table, and patted Cardozo's shoulder.

"Excellent, detective constable first class. You have now managed to link Gabrielle with both the baboon and Francesco Pullini. Three suspects, one woman, two men, and each man has a sexual relationship with the woman. A lot of loose pieces should fit in now, all we have to do is find out how." He waved for the bill. "Well, Grijpstra, how about your theory? I'm sure you and the sergeant have worked out an angle from which Mrs. Carnet's death could be explained. Is your theory still standing?"

Grijpstra touched de Gier's sleeve. De Gier was staring

at the black girl at the other table.

"Yes," de Gier said, "yes, sir. The theory still stands, but it isn't strong enough to hold a suspect. I was thinking of doing some more work, tomorrow morning. I can't do it tonight."

The commissaris paid the bill and complimented the Chinese on the quality of his food. He got up, scraping his chair energetically, but bent down to feel his thigh. His thin lips tightened.

"I won't ask you what your theory is, sergeant. I have my own, but it doesn't stand up too well either as yet. I'll have to go further too. I may be away tomorrow, possibly the day after tomorrow. Meanwhile you can go ahead, but I would appreciate your not making an arrest until I'm back. Ideally our theories should be identical and we should arrive at the same results, but we have been pushing the case and perhaps we should go slower now."

His pale eyes made contact with each of the three men in turn.

"Good."

The dog was licking her private parts again as they left the restaurant. Cardozo tripped over her and stumbled into the prostitutes' table. The black girl caught him.

"Clumsy fellow, aren't you?" de Gier asked.

Grijpstra grinned. "Ignore him, Cardozo. I've seen the sergeant make such a mess here once that it took two waiters an hour to clean up after him." Cardozo looked grateful.

"I was making an arrest then," de Gier said. "You always tell part of the story. We were trying to catch a fellow with a knife as long as your arm."

"Tut-tut-tut."

"Did he have a knife or didn't he?"

"We each had a pistol."

"Gentlemen," the commissaris said from the open doorway, "it's getting late. The door is open, there is a draft, the ladies will catch cold."

"Sir," they said as they trooped into the street.

15

It was nearly eleven o'clock when the commissaris came home and his wife was waiting for him in the corridor.

"Dear . . ."

"Yes?"

"You shouldn't be out so late. I wish you would stay in, at least during the evening. You know what the doctor said."

"Yes. Rest. But I did rest."

"Just for two days, he said two weeks. Your bath will be ready in a few minutes."

"Good, any messages?"

"Just one, a telephone call at nine o'clock. A Mr. de Bree."

"You have the number?"

She pointed to the pad next to the telephone and he walked over to it and began to dial.

"Mr. de Bree?"

"Commissaris, I would like to come and see you if possible, something has come up."

"You could tell me over the telephone."

There was a pause. "I would rather come and see you. I have some information."

"Now?"

"I can be with you in five minutes, I have my car."

"Very well."

The commissaris hung up. His wife was standing next to him, her arm around his shoulders. "Please, dear, not now, call him and tell him to come tomorrow. You've had such a long day and you look so pale. Why don't you go and have your bath, surely the matter can wait till tomorrow."

"No, dear, it's a bad case and I've been pushing it, it's my own fault. The man won't stay long, I promise."

The doorbell rang and the commissaris peeked from behind a curtain before he went to open the door. Mr. de Bree had arrived in a brand-new Mercedes and had left the car in the driveway. He had forgotten to close the car door and its lights were on.

The bell rang again. The commissaris didn't hurry. He opened the door and looked down on de Bree's sweaty, bare skull, gleaming under the light of the driveway's lantern.

"Yes, Mr. de Bree?"

"I'm sorry to bother you at this hour, sir, but my information may be of interest to you and I thought . . ."

"That's quite all right, I hadn't gone to bed yet. Please come in."

They walked through the long corridor and the commissaris led the way into his study. It was a hot evening and the garden doors were still open.

"Perhaps we can sit outside, it'll be pleasant in the garden."

They faced each other in two old cane chairs. The commissaris offered his flat tin and lit his visitor's cigar. De Bree puffed nervously.

"You said you had some information?"

"Yes. You remember Paul, the terrier that belongs to the Carnets?"

"The information has to do with the dog?"

"No, but . . ."

De Bree's cigar showed a red-hot end; the commissaris

144

could hear the tobacco crackle as more air was sucked into it.

"Go ahead, Mr. de Bree, take your time."

"The dog. I went to see my lawyer as you suggested and he says it is a bad business . . ."

"It *is* a bad business, Mr. de Bree."

"Yes. Quite. But I have some information, as I said just now, and it has to do with Mrs. Carnet's death. My lawyer said I should give it to you and . . ."

"Maybe I would forget about the bad business with the dog?"

"Yes." De Bree looked much relieved. He was smiling broadly. The glowing cigar hung in his limp head.

The commissaris's thin eyebrows met above the bridge of his nose. "No. Absolutely not. We won't forget about Paul. You'll go to court, Mr. de Bree, and get your verdict. And I still want your information. If you don't give it you will be in even more trouble. I am surprised your lawyer didn't tell you that. I am sure he *did* tell you but perhaps you weren't listening. If you have information that concerns the Carnet death, and if a crime is involved in that death—and there *is* a crime involved, I assure you, Mr. de Bree—and if you withhold that information, then you are committing a crime yourself."

De Bree was sucking on his cigar again. "Really?"

"Yes. Absolutely."

"But if I don't tell you about what I saw then there is no information, commissaris. You won't know what I saw. Maybe I saw nothing. You can't accuse me because of something that does not exist."

"Your information does exist. You have told me twice already, once when I opened the door for you and once just now. Beg your pardon, you told me three times. You also told me on the phone. I am a police officer, I don't need witnesses. If I write a report and state that you told me three times that you had information about the Carnet death and that you refused to give it to me afterward, then you are withholding evidence and my report, signed under oath, will be irrefutable proof, acceptable to the court."

"Is that so?" de Bree asked softly.

There was an uneasy silence, accentuated by a slight rustle as a turtle came out of the weeds near the commissaris's feet. De Bree looked down at the small armored creature that was plodding steadily forward. "A turtle!"

"He lives here. Well, Mr. de Bree?"

De Bree breathed out sharply; his nostrils widened and pointed threateningly, like the barrels of a miniature shotgun.

"Very well. That night, the night of the gale, the night of Mrs. Carnet's death, I was in my garden. I was looking for Tobias. He hadn't come in, and I was also worried about the trees, a lot of trees fell that night. While I was outside I heard a terrible screaming and shouting coming from Mrs. Carnet's porch. There were several people shouting at the same time, but her voice was the loudest. I couldn't hear what she said, but she appeared to be hysterical, completely out of control. And then the door of her porch opened and I saw her fall. She had a flowered dress on, which made her body stand out against the lights coming from the porch. Mrs. Carnet fell with such force that she must have been pushed, 'shoved' might be a better word. She came hurtling down and a man fell with her. He rolled over her, it seemed. He was holding on to her, so he must have pushed her to the door and the momentum of his push made him fall with her. I saw the two at the top of the stairs. I couldn't see the complete fall for there were bushes in the way, and the hedge and some small trees, and the gale was blowing everything about. It happened very quickly, of course. There were more than two people in the Carnet house for I saw a shadow, a silhouette, move behind the windows of the porch, not very clearly, again, for there are curtains that are draped in such a way that more than half the surface of the windows is obscured."

"Did you see the man who fell with Mrs. Carnet go back into the house again?"

"Yes. He was in pain. He was dragging himself up."

"Big man? Small man? Did you recognize him?"

"I didn't know him. He didn't seem too big, but there

was some distance and I couldn't see too clearly. I had seen enough anyway. I went back into my house after that. Tobias had shown up and I didn't want to hang around.''

"Didn't you realize that what you had seen made you a valuable witness to a crime?''

De Bree shrugged. "Who wants to be a witness? It's a lot of bother. You have to go to court and waste a lot of time, and some shyster tries to ask smart questions and show you up for a nitwitted fool. What other people do is other people's concern. I hardly knew the Carnets. Maybe they were having a party. And you mustn't forget that I had no idea Mrs. Carnet was dead, I thought she just fell, twisted her ankle perhaps. There aren't all that many steps to the stairs in these gardens. And if she had been in trouble the other people with her would have helped her.''

"You knew there had been a crime later, when you learned that we had initiated an investigation.''

De Bree wiped his face. "Yes, perhaps, but then you had got to me too, about the dog. I didn't want to attract any more attention to myself until my lawyer suggested . . .''

"I see. How was the man who fell with Mrs. Carnet dressed?''

"I don't remember. I saw a dark shape going down with her. It looked male. I think it wore a dark jacket, but ladies also wear dark jackets. Come to think of it now, I couldn't even swear in court that the shape was male.''

"And who was left on the porch? Male or female?''

"Female, I think, but there again I can't be sure, for I only had a glimpse of something moving. But there had been a man involved in the fight, for when the screaming was going on there was a male voice.''

"You say you didn't hear any words. Do you remember what language they were screaming in?''

"No. Dutch, I imagine, but I'm not sure. Mrs. Carnet is French, isn't she? Originally, I mean?''

"Belgian, but she did speak French.''

De Bree got up. The turtle had reached a large rock and was standing against it, nibbling at a lettuce leaf that had been put out on a tray.

"Your pet?"

"Yes, and it doesn't chase cats, all it does is try to destroy my wife's herb garden."

De Bree smiled ruefully. "I really am sorry about that business with Paul, you know."

The commissaris smiled back. "I am sure, Mr. de Bree, and I hope your regret will show in court. Don't forget to offer to pay damages before the judge mentions it, but I think your lawyer has given you the same advice already."

"Your bath," his wife said as he came back from the front door.

"Yes. But I want to phone the airport. I'll be flying to Italy tomorrow, dear, a nice easy trip. I won't be long, a day and a night at the most."

"Oh . . ."

"Did you run the bath?" He was on his way up the stairs. "And by the way, did you remember to buy that cane?"

"Yes."

"Would you show it to me?"

She went into the living room and came back carrying a bamboo cane with a silver handle.

"Very nice, just what I had in mind. I'll take it to Italy with me. This limp is beginning to be a nuisance. I can still hide it at headquarters where the doctor can see me but I think I'll use the cane whenever I'm sure he isn't around. I'll keep it in the car, it'll be safe there."

His wife began to cry. "You're an invalid now, darling, you should really retire. I can't stand it, the way you're killing yourself. I'll go anywhere with you, I really don't mind leaving Amsterdam. We can go to that strange island, Curaçao, the place you're always talking about. That's in the tropics, isn't it? Your legs won't hurt over there."

He came down the stairs and took the cane from her hand and leaned on it, embracing her with his free arm.

"I love you, but you would be very unhappy if you had to leave Amsterdam now. All your relatives and friends are here. Later, maybe, we'll discuss it. This cane will be a lot of help."

They stood for a while, leaning against each other, until he slipped away and began to climb the stairs again.

"The bath," he said softly, "it'll get cold. And I would love some tea. Let's have tea together. I'll soak and you'll sit and watch me soak."

16

Amsterdam dropped away as the plane banked, and the commissaris admired the pale greens and faded blues of fields and ponds set apart by geometrical patterns of expressways spreading out from the city. He had observed the tall suburban apartment buildings rising from parks as they swept away under the roaring jet engines. Their disappearance evoked some satisfaction. He was traveling, getting away, even if it was only for a moment. His forehead rested against the window as the plane flew above a large swamp. He knew the swamp well. It had been a mysterious world once, an endless maze of lagoons and reed-lined twisted ditches filled with murky water. He remembered the freshwater kelp that waved and intertwined in the depth, moved by hidden currents or the undulating sleek bodies of pikes and eels. The swamp had provided his first real discovery, a first indication that there was more to life than school and trying to find ways to fit in with what grownups wanted him to do in the boring grayness of the small provincial town where he was raised.

He craned his neck but the swamp had gone while the plane gained more height and broke through the clouds and reached the great transparency of the sky. It occurred to him that the sky is an emptiness that sits on a layer of cotton wool and has no limit, an ungraspable manifestation of the mystery that he had also felt as a ten-year-old boy, exploring swamp backwaters in a canoe. The swamp had revealed some of its wonders then, the sky might do the same. And he was in it now, reclining in a first-class seat, reaching the top of a curve that would soon begin to dip down again and take him back to the twisted failings of humanity. Afloat in the universe and free while it lasted. Not a bad thought.

A stewardess bent down and smiled professionally. Did the gentleman want a drink? But surely, a nice cold old Dutch gin. He felt supremely happy as he sipped the icy, syrupy liquid and he grinned, for he had remembered what the blond baboon had said the day before. Happiness is a silly word because it has to do with security and security does not exist. True, of course. There is no absolute security and happiness is silly. How very clever of the baboon to have seen that. But there is temporary security and therefore temporary happiness does exist. Right now he was temporarily happy, and temporarily free of everything that annoyed or threatened him. Afloat in the universe. He mumbled the words, swallowed the gin, smacked his lips, and closed his eyes. He was asleep when the stewardess touched his shoulder.

"Yes?"

"We have arrived, sir."

"Ah."

He followed her, carrying his small overnight bag and the bamboo cane with the silver handle.

Giovanni Pullini's foot kicked an empty matchbox rather viciously. He had been waiting for a while near the airport's security barrier, guarded by two carabinieri. The carabinieri clutched short-barreled machine guns, and their dark eyes, in which passion and ferocity were equally mixed, scanned the crowd of incoming passengers. One of the passengers would be the commissaris de la police municipale d'Amsterdam, whom Giovanni Pullini had been talking to two hours before. He had no idea what the man looked like but knew that the foreign policeman would be carrying a cane. Pullini didn't know what the commissaris wanted although he could guess. Pullini didn't like guessing. A vague but sensuous smile lifted his mouth as a bevy of stewardesses pranced past in high heels, bosoms raised, eyelashes flapping rhythmically

The smirk faded as his predicament flashed through his mind again. His wide shoulders bulged under his custom-made sharkskin jacket and his short squat body moved a little closer to the barrier His long eyebrows frowned above the deep-set eyes in a round red face. He felt his balding head. His head wasn't of much use to him now. It was only telling him that he might be in trouble, real trouble, and he hadn't been in real trouble for a long time. The opposite was true, he had been doing very well. And he shouldn't be at the airport now, it was lunchtime, he should be in the country restaurant he owned. He should be listening to Renata, the charming lady who ran the restaurant and who lived in the beautifully furnished apartment on its second floor, an apartment he was getting to know better than his own house. A commissaris with a cane. He saw an old man, a thin little old man, limping toward the barrier The devil himself, the devil in paradise.

Pullini's smile was soft and charming when he shook hands and took the commissaris's overnight bag.

"You had a good flight, commissaire?"

"Yes, thank you. I slept"

A few minutes later they sat on the rear seat of a large car, a new car of a make the commissaris didn't recognize. The limousine was chauffeured by a dreamy young man in a turtleneck sweater of exactly the same tender blue shade as the car.

Pullini pulled down the armrest and his strong, suntanned hand, adorned with two rings, each holding a large diamond, dug into its soft upholstery The commissaris's eyes flitted up and observed Pullini's face. Pullini's heavy thoughts were filling the car The commissaris was thinking too He had planned his attack early that morning, in the garden with the turtle rummaging around his feet and his wife fussing in the kitchen, coming out every ten minutes to refill his coffee cup. He had looked forward to meeting Papa Pullini, but now that his prey was next to him, breathing heavily through nostrils bristling with long dark hairs, he didn't feel like upsetting the man. Perhaps some rapport had been established between the two, for Pullini's face turned slowly and his lips formed a single word.

"Non?"

"Non."

Pullini's grip on the armrest loosened.

"We go to hotel now. In Sesto San Giovanni. Saint Giovanni. Same name as me, but me no saint." He laughed and the commissaris laughed too. A joke.

"Small hotel. Comfortable. One night, yes?"

"One night."

"You have bath, sleep a little, go for a walk maybe, and then I come and we drink some wine. Good wine. Later we eat, we talk."

Pullini's smile was innocent, childlike, and hurt the commissaris. He was sure that Pullini had tried to contact his son immediately after their conversation of that morning. But there hadn't been much time. Chances were that Pullini still knew very little. He would know about Mrs. Carnet's death, for Francesco would have reported such an important event in the connection between the Pullini and Carnet firms.

"Did you speak to your son this morning, Mr. Pullini?"

"I try. I phone hotel. I phone Carnet and Company. Francesco, he not there. I want to ask Francesco what happened that is so important that Amsterdam police commissaire comes to see me in Milano. Police, they do not like to spend money, yes?"

"Yes."

Pullini was holding his smile. The smile displayed a glitter of gold and very white artificial teeth, well made and suitably irregular. He raised his hands. "Commissaire, I know nothing."

"Do you know what happened to Mrs. Carnet?"

The red face froze. "Yes. She dead. Francesco, he tell

me. An accident, yes? Or maybe no? You do not travel to Italy for accident."

An enormous truck pulling an equally enormous trailer zoomed past blasting its horn. The limousine's chauffeur flicked his wheel. His employee's equanimity seemed to calm Pullini.

"O.K."

The word was out of place between the gigantic billboards screaming their advertising in poetic, flowing Italian on both sides of the autostrada.

The car turned off the main road and began to follow a narrow cobblestoned path winding through fields planted with ripening corn. The nondescript office and factory buildings that had lined the autostrada gave way to long cracked-tiled divisions screening the rustic peace of the countryside. There were rows of high trees, a dam with a waterwheel, and a high bridge that had to be negotiated in low gear. The commissaris saw farmhouses built like low, square fortresses defending themselves behind forbidding walls, centered on courtyards overshadowed by umbrella-shaped chestnuts and tall poplars.

Pullini pointed out a low pink and gray building. "There I was born, not farmer's son, laborer's son, in shed. Shed no longer there. Burned in war."

The simple elements that formed Pullini's face proved to be capable of forming fairly complicated expressions, even combinations of opposites such as sadness and triumph.

"You were happy on the farm, Mr. Pullini?"

"No. My father, he works. My mother, she works. Me, I also work. Always. Feed pigs, shovel shit, pigshit, cowshit, horseshit. Also chickenshit. Chickenshit, he worse. Chickenshit, he burns. All in same wheelbarrow. Wheelbarrow bad. Push like this."

Pullini leaned over and groaned, trying to hold the wheelbarrow.

"Sometimes it falls over. Then I shovel same shit twice." He held up two fingers. "But I had birds. Pheasants. Partridges. Beautiful birds. They walk around like this: titch-titch-titch. Baby birds.''

His hand moved around on the floor of the car, making short, swift movements. ''When they grow I sell to farmer. Farmer, he eats my birds. But every year new nests and new birds. One year I buy peacock, but only money for one, so no baby peacocks. Farmer, he takes peacock.''

''Did he pay you?''

Pullini laughed, a soft full bellylaugh that gurgled in his throat. ''No. Farmer says peacock eats too much feed so he takes him for courtyard. Farmer looks at peacock, me, I listen. Peacock shouts, 'Giovanni! Giovanni!' and I listen. Then I know one day Pullini must work for Pullini. That better.''

The car turned sharply. They had come to a village. A man greeted the car, then two women who came out of a store, then another man from the doorway of a shop. The greetings were elaborate. The subjects waved and inclined their heads respectfully. Pullini raised his hand but he didn't wave. He only showed his hand. The driver also reacted by lifting a finger of the hand holding the wheel. The car's nose pointed at a three-story brick building and stopped. A neon sign above the building's double front door said RISTORANTE PULLINI.

''Very nice.'' The commissaris pointed at the sign. ''You have another restaurant, I hear, in the mountains somewhere, I believe?''

''Who tell you?'' Pullini's chest bent over the armrest; a whiff of garlic touched the commissaris's face. ''My son?''

''Mr. Bergen told me.''

Pullini's gold fillings flashed. ''Yes. Bergen, he eats very much, but kitchen has plenty of spaghetti, plenty of sauce, plenty of sausage. Also veal, tender veal from Holland, many lires a gram. Bergen, he likes meat. That restaurant in mountains same as this one here, same kitchen. This cook, he teaches cook in mountains. Before, restaurants were bad, just one dish, spaghetti and tomato sauce and sometimes fish, old fish. Now better. We try later tonight, yes?''

The car moved again, following a narrow side street with only centimeters to spare on each side, and emerged into a small sunlit square. A policeman in an olive uniform and carrying a gigantic sidearm in a dazzlingly white gunbelt came to attention. Pullini got out and shook the constable's hand. The driver slid from behind the wheel. The commissaris rested on his cane. The square was quiet, medievally quiet, paved with gleaming yellow stones, dappled by the light caught and softened in the foliage of protecting oaks. Shrubs grew in enclaves on the narrow pavement and songbirds chirped from cages hung under the arc of a gate.

Pullini's hand nudged his elbow and the commissaris remembered his business.

"Yes, thank you, Mr. Pullini. What do you think about Mr. Bergen?"

"Bergen," Pullini said, feeling the word with his thick lips. "Bergen, he all right. He buyer, I seller. He buys, he pays. Sometimes he pays late, and Francesco telephones and talks about this and that and then Francesco says 'Money' and Bergen, he pays. And sometimes he comes here."

"You think he is a good businessman?"

"Half."

"Half?"

"Half. Bergen is salesman. Big salesman, not big buyer. He, how do you say?" Pullini tried some Italian words and the commissaris held up his hands in apologetic despair. "You don't understand, no? Here." Pullini breathed in and his chest swelled up. He kept his breath. A foolish grin spread over his face and his eyes narrowed.

"I see," the commissaris said gratefully. "A showoff. He tries to impress, is that it?"

Pullini breathed out. "Yes. But Bergen all right as long as he pays. That other man, he better. I forget name of other man." Pullini bent and swung his arms. His lips pouted. He frowned.

"Mr. Vleuten?"

"Yes. The monkeyman. He better. But he gone now. One time Francesco thinks maybe monkeyman he marries

Mrs. Carnet and take business. Vleuten, he good business-man. Bergen, he sells, to anybody, any price. Like Francesco, but Francesco, he learns, he changes. Bergen, he never learns.''

They had arrived at the hotel. Pullini had puffed himself up again and was strutting around the car's bumper, leading the way to the hotel. The commissaris followed slowly. Pullini waited.

"And Gabrielle Carnet, what do you think of her, Mr. Pullini?"

Pullini's face fell. "Me, I don't know Gabrielle. Francesco, he likes her. Gabrielle, she beautiful, yes?"

The commissaris nodded firmly. "Yes. She is."

Pullini whistled. The butt of the small cigar the commissaris had given him rolled on his underlip. He scratched his nose.

"Now maybe Carnet and Company finished."

"Possibly."

"Never mind. We find other company, Holland has many companies. Pullini furniture is good, good quality, good price. Maybe I go to Holland now. Set up own office. Find good Dutchman, good Dutchman he becomes manager. Holland has many good Dutchmen. Maybe you help me, yes? You and I, do a little business?"

The owner of the hotel had come into the street to meet Pullini and the two men embraced. The commissaris was introduced with a flourish and the owner took the overnight bag from Pullini's hand. His bow to the commissaris showed servility, deep friendship, respect, and a great love. His smile flashed as he straightened up again. They were ushered into the building with another display of exuberant intimacy. The commissaris's room on the second floor was large. It had a floor of marble slabs and deep windows, each window with its own vase holding matched bouquets of wildflowers. The owner pointed at the bed as if he wanted to excuse its poor appearance but the bed was big and sumptuous, with clean crisp sheets and a stack of downy pillows. The posts of the brass frame were crowned with white and blue ceramic balls.

"Lovely," the commissaris said, and Pullini translated and patted the owner on the back. The owner pulled his drooping mustache and hunched in a tremendous effort to comment on the compliment. He found a word: "Happy!"

"Yes. Happy."

The commissaris and the owner beamed at each other. The owner opened a door and showed the bathroom. More marble, once white but aged to a delicate shade of ivory. A tub with brass faucets. A brass tank resting on solid oak.

"Hot," the owner said proudly.

Pullini and the owner linked arms and marched to the door. They bowed together. "I come back seven o'clock. O.K.?"

"O.K., Mr. Pullini."

"Have bath, sleep, then walk. Sesto San Giovanni very small, can't get lost."

"Sure. Thank you."

The commissaris sighed as he lowered himself into the bath. His legs felt like two thin dry sticks that had been thrown into a roaring fire. The steaming water would calm the pain once more. A maid had brought a pot of strong tea and he poured himself a cup that rested on the tiled rim of the bath. He forced himself not to think of further developments and made pleasurable little noises instead as the water swept along his legs and hips and reached his chest and shoulders. He even sang, a wordless song consisting of grunts that lengthened and flowed into each other. He sipped his tea and stopped singing. The case had grabbed his mind again and the image of Papa Pullini dominated the stage of his brain.

If only Papa Pullini had married Elaine Carnet. But perhaps it had been too much to expect. A young Italian businessman romancing with a nightclub singer in Paris. All very well. But she gets pregnant. The young Italian businessman fades away. The months pass. The beautiful nightclub singer doesn't sing anymore. She watches her body grow in an upstairs bedroom in Amsterdam. She writes letters on blue perfumed paper. There is an answer, on the Pullini furniture company's letterhead. It is not a romantic letter. It avoids the subject of pregnancy and it doesn't mention the matter of marriage. It offers an agency in furniture. The commissaris's hand came down and hit the bath water. For God's sake! What a way to handle the problem. But a way that suited Papa Pullini's temperament and it had worked. He didn't know how it had worked and he would probably never find out. Had Elaine left her baby in the care of a relative or paid help and traveled through Holland by train and visited the big stores? Had she shown her prospective customers a catalogue and a price list or had she organized a showroom somewhere and enticed clients to look at her wares? The preposterous fact was that Carnet and Company was born together with Gabrielle. He hit the water again with such force that some of it splashed into his teacup. He put the cup into the tub and pushed it around. Papa Pullini had been very clever and very businesslike but it would have been better if he had married Elaine, for if he had Francesco wouldn't have pushed his father's former mistress down the garden stairs of her house in the Mierisstraat. A long chain of events crinkling through a space of thirty years, but set off by Papa Pullini's brilliant egotism.

He imagined the final scene, knowing that he had to be very close to the truth, that he might as well have been in the room, together with Gabrielle, who saw her lover and half-brother kill her mother. Manslaughter, of course, provoked manslaughter, there had been no premeditation in the act. He saw Elaine Carnet, dowdy and painted to hide the lines and folds caused by loneliness and bitter thoughts and continuous frustration. Drunk, most likely. And angry, vengeful. Convinced of her right, snarling with victory. She had been waiting for Francesco, she had probably telephoned him at his hotel. She had created the situation and was, finally, in charge of her circumstances. Francesco had come for one simple reason, his eighty thousand guilders that Bergen hadn't paid and that he couldn't tell Papa Pullini about, for Papa Pullini didn't know that his son had organized a private commission on all sales to the Dutch firm. Francesco didn't know why Elaine Carnet wanted to give him the money instead of Bergen and he didn't care, all

Francesco wanted was his cash.

He had gone as a helpless beggar and he must have been in a foul mood. Bergen had been threatening not to give him any more orders. The business might be ending then and there. His trip to Amsterdam had turned into a nightmare. He wasn't feeling well either, he was sniffling and sneezing. And instead of handing him a discreet brown envelope to be stuffed into his inside pocket Mrs. Carnet had been waving the money at him, a thick wad of thousand-guilder notes, a small fortune that he desperately needed to pay for his expensive private pleasures. She had screamed. It had taken him awhile to understand what she was screaming about, but it became clear soon enough. She was explaining, in French, and at the top of her voice, that Papa Pullini was Gabrielle's father and that he hadn't married her but had made her work for him instead, to enlarge the Pullini business. That there had been no choice. That she had had to give Papa Pullini business to pay for the upbringing and education of his own child, Gabrielle, Francesco's half-sister. That she had known, all along, that Francesco and Gabrielle were having an affair, that history was repeating itself. That she knew that Francesco had married in Italy, a rich girl with the right connections, just as his father had done twenty-odd years ago.

Francesco hadn't answered her. He had sat in his chair, his handsome bearded head resting on his slender hands. He had wanted her to stop screaming. But she went on and on, repeating herself, waving the money, dropping some of it and picking it up again. She wasn't going to give it to him. She was only showing it. She would keep it as a small repayment for a lot of suffering. It was hers. Money squeezed out of the pockets of Italian lovers who took their girls for long walks in the moonlight, who sent flowers and beautifully wrapped presents, who slithered into the girls' beds and who performed so admirably only to slide away in the night if the relationships proved to yield more problems than pleasures.

The gale shrieked around the house as Francesco sat listening and the woman screamed on, her lips bubbling with venom. And when she paused it was only to remember swear words in both French and Italian, flinging them at him as they came to her. She had taken off her wedding ring, wrenching it off her finger. She threw it on the floor and it rolled toward his feet and he stared at it. Francesco was having difficulty understanding Mrs. Carnet. His French was bad, but he did know some words, and he gradually began to fit together what the crazy woman was telling him. His nerves stretched even more tautly as a fresh torrent of abuse burst free. Mrs. Carnet's voice had dropped now; she was whispering and her insults had the sharpness of a dagger. The dagger slid into his feverish, aching brain.

"But times have changed," Mrs. Carnet was whispering. Oh yes, times had changed. Girls were no longer helpless and had woken up to the hardness and cruelty of the male world that would use and manipulate and discard them if it was given half a chance. Papa Pullini hadn't liked to use anything when he made love and neither would Francesco. Men didn't like a film of rubber to come between them and their pleasure. They wanted all their pleasure, and if their pleasure led to their girlfriends' sorrow, well, what of it? They were up and away, hunting for fresh game. But now girls had the pill and they didn't get pregnant unless they wanted to. And girls had many lovers now, as many as they pleased.

Did Francesco know that he was only one of Gabrielle's lovers? That Gabrielle only accepted his embraces because he happened to please her for the time being? Other men were asked to come to Gabrielle's apartment upstairs, and they were told to go when she no longer needed them. Gabrielle didn't care so much about Francesco. Gabrielle didn't even care that Francesco was her half-brother. For she knew. She had been told, just now, just a few days ago. Francesco could go back to Italy and never come back and Gabrielle would replace him, just like *that*. And Mrs. Carnet stepped forward, leering, and snapped her fingers in his face.

And it was the last thing she ever did, for Francesco jumped her and tore the money out of her hand and pushed her to the open garden door. They fell together and Francesco came back alone, to face Gabrielle, who hadn't moved from her corner throughout her mother's final performance. They had probably gone down into the garden together and ascertained Mrs. Carnet's death. Perhaps Francesco had cried and Gabrielle had comforted him, she might have stroked his hair. Perhaps Gabrielle had hated her mother and pitied her half-brother. Perhaps she had always wanted a brother and her love could have changed but not ended.

The commissaris pushed the teacup; it filled with soapy water and sank onto his legs. Gabrielle still had a portrait in her room, close to her pillow, that resembled Francesco's features. What did he know about a woman's love? Gabrielle also loved the baboon, for she carried his omen, his symbol, between her breasts. She might have protected Francesco out of love, but it could also be that she was levelheaded enough not to want the police to meddle with someone who was her lover, her brother, and an important business contact, the man who controlled the supplies of furniture that her firm depended on. Whatever her motives, she had covered up the mess, removed Francesco's glass, wiped everything his hands might have touched, and sent him back to his hotel. She hadn't telephoned the police but the ambulance service, hoping that her mother's death would be filed away as accidental.

And she had allowed him to leave with the money but had probably contacted him again later, very likely early in the next morning, and arranged for him to return the cash so that she could pretend to find it. And Francesco had been honest enough to return the full hundred thousand. That Mrs. Carnet had waved a hundred notes at him instead of the eighty she owed would have been due to her state of nerves. She had simply added the twenty notes she had just received from the baboon, perhaps to make the wad thicker and more impressive.

Perhaps Gabrielle was a courageous girl who should be allowed to take care of her own life and not be charged as an accomplice to a serious crime. But as the killer's half-sister she might be excused, although she would be charged. The commissaris looked at the submerged cup and thought of refloating it but began to climb out of the tub instead. He wouldn't let Francesco off, for Francesco had pushed a lady down her own garden stairs and the lady had broken her neck. The young man should have had the sense to confess, but he might still be manipulated into a confession. It would help his case and soften the lesson. And this trip was part of that manipulation, but so far it had only resulted in a pleasant hour in a marble bathtub. He found his watch and began to dress. There was still plenty of time. He would go for a walk.

The commissaris had walked for no more than a quarter of an hour when he found himself on a long narrow road with a low wall on each side. He had come to the end of the village and the road was leading to a confusion of small fields, all carefully planted with vegetables. He had just decided to turn back when he saw a small green truck roaring around the next curve. A disreputable pickup with a snarling, lopsided grille set between rusted headlights that wobbled on dented mudguards. As the truck hurtled toward him he recognized its driver, a young man in a light blue turtleneck sweater, the same imperturbable young man who had driven Pullini's limousine. He thought of raising his hand in greeting when he realized that the pickup was coming straight at him, that its left wheels were on the sidewalk, and that its mudguard was razing the crumbling wall. The pickup was sounding its hoarse little horn, but there was nowhere for the commissaris to go, and he pointed his cane at it in a futile gesture of defiance.

17

Sergeant de Gier looked at the square electric wall clock that had been hanging, for as long as he could remember, on an improbably thin and bent nail stuck loosely into the soft plaster of his office wall. The clock had said five to eight and had just moved, with an ominous faint click, to four to eight.

"It's morning," he said, and his voice reverberated through the empty room. The hollow, artificial sound sent a shiver through the base of his neck. "It's *very* early in the morning," he whispered. There had been no coffee in the machine in the washroom and he was out of cigarettes. The cigarette machine in the hall was out of order. The tobacconist's wouldn't open up until after nine. Cardozo and his plastic pouch filled with crumbly, cheap, shag tobacco were nowhere to be seen. Grijpstra and his flat tin of cigars hadn't come in yet. The commissaris's office was securely locked. There was nothing to do but to stare at the clock and at his desk calendar, which showed no entries at all.

"First things first," de Gier said and jumped up. He had heard a sound in the corridor. He pulled the door open and jumped out and collided with a uniformed secretary from the traffic department. Her blue jacket showed the stripes of a constable.

"Darling," de Gier murmured, and he clasped the dumpy girl in his arms and breathed against her thick spectacles. "You smoke, don't you? Tell me you do."

The constable had dropped her shoulderbag; her spectacles were sliding down her short broad nose.

"Yes," she said into de Gier's shoulder. "Yes, I do, sergeant."

"Half a pack," he whispered. "Give me half a pack and maybe I can do some work today. Catch the horrible killer, grab the pernicious poisoner, trap the blond baboon. Please? Beloved?"

Her glasses dropped, but he extended his chest, and they caught on the top button of his jacket. He plucked them away, released the girl, whipped out his handkerchief, and polished them before replacing them gently onto her nose and sliding the stems over her ears.

"You shouldn't do that," the girl said. "You are a pig, sergeant." Her breathing was still irregular but her tight little smile had a hard twist to it. "So you're out of cigarettes?"

"Yes, darling," de Gier said, "and I caught your spectacles. They would have broken if I hadn't caught them and you would have been blind as a bat, they would have smashed to smithereens on the nasty floor."

"I won't give you any cigarettes," she said firmly, "unless . . ."

"I'll kiss you," de Gier said. "How's that?"

"On your knees!"

"What?"

"On your knees!"

De Gier looked around. There was nobody in sight in the long corridor. He dropped onto his knees.

"Repeat after me: 'I am a male chauvinist!' "

"I am a male chauvinist."

She opened her bag and took out a pack of cigarettes. De Gier looked at the brand. It was the wrong brand. Long and thin and low on tar and tasteless with holed filters that would let the smoke drift away before it could reach his mouth. His lips curled down, but she was watching his face, so he smiled pleasingly.

"I'll give you four, that's all you're worth." She counted them out on his palm.

"Well, well, *well*," Grijpstra said.

The girl was on her way, her heels tapping firmly on the thick linoleum of the corridor. De Gier had got up.

"Well what, adjutant? I was out of cigarettes."

Grijpstra's grin was still spreading. "Ha!"

"Ha what, adjutant?"

"Pity Cardozo wasn't here. There he is! Late again, always late."

Cardozo looked at his watch. "Five to nine, adjutant."

"Never mind."

They went in together. Cardozo was sent out to buy coffee and to pay for it out of his own pocket. De Gier puffed on his cigarette, threw it on the floor, and stamped on it. Cardozo came back.

"Give me your pouch, Cardozo, and some cigarette paper and a light."

Cardozo put the coffee mugs down and fished a crumpled plastic pouch of shag tobacco from his pocket. "Do you want me to smoke it for you too, sergeant?"

De Gier reached out and took the pouch. The three men smoked and drank coffee and stared at each other. Grijpstra sighed. "Well . . ."

"Yes?"

"It seems the case is solved. I saw the commissaris's secretary just now. The old man has gone to Milano, he's due back tomorrow. He telephoned her last night and wanted Papa Pullini's number in Sesto San Giovanni, a little town close to Milano. The round-trip ticket to Milano must cost a bit of money and he wouldn't be wasting it, would he now?"

De Gier stretched and began to cough. He glared at Cardozo. "Terrible tobacco, you should change your brand." Cardozo tried to say something but winced instead.

"Right," de Gier said. "So Francesco is our man, as we

thought, but there's still a chance that we're wrong, for the commissaris could be wrong too.''

Grijpstra yawned.

''Small chance, but still . . . Let's go through it again: Why did we pick Francesco?''

''We picked Francesco,'' Grijpstra said patiently, ''for a number of reasons, all of them flimsy and none of them good enough to stand up in court.''

''Let's have the reasons.''

''O.K. We agreed that whoever smokes long thin cigars with plastic mouthpieces made to resemble ivory must be a vain man. We had three suspects, apart from Gabrielle. All the suspects were vain.. Bergen is a nicely dressed gentleman if he isn't going to pieces in the privacy of his own home. The baboon is a strange-looking man, but he takes great care about the way he looks, and Francesco dries and sets his lovely hair with a dryer and sports a silk dressing gown. All three suspects are vain, but Francesco wins the race. A very faint hint, but something to go on if we can bring up supporting hints.

''A man who pushes a lady down the stairs is violent. We couldn't picture Bergen pushing Elaine and we had trouble imagining the baboon in that position. The baboon is violent, for he got you in the river, but you are a man, not a nicely dressed lady in her own house. Francesco could be an excitable young fellow and he had some sort of a motive. He thought the Carnet firm owed him eighty thousand guilders and we knew that Elaine Carnet took out eighty thousand in cash from her company's bank account. The figures tally, she had the money the evening of her death, and Francesco could have visited her. Suppose she showed him the money but wouldn't give it to him so he jumps her, right?''

''Hmm.''

''It was your idea,'' Grijpstra said, ''and I agreed with it. Eighty thousand guilders form a motive. What motives could Bergen and the baboon have?''

''The wedding ring.''

''Yes, sergeant, a powerful indication, A wedding ring

on the floor and the lady was never married. Yet she wore a ring. And she threw it on the floor that evening; it didn't just drop off her finger. Marriage, love or the lack of love."

"Humiliation," de Gier said.

"Exactly. Women like to humiliate men these days. You were on the corridor's floor a little while ago, groveling. You wanted a cigarette, I believe, and the girl was using her power."

"What?" Cardozo had jumped up. "The sergeant on the floor? What happened?"

"If you had been on time you would have seen what was happening. A female constable had our sergeant on the floor, on his knees, whining."

"Really?"

"Let it go," de Gier said, "I was only play-acting. You're right about the humiliation. So you're saying that Elaine Carnet had her future killer in a position where he felt silly and his pathetic predicament had something to do with her wedding ring. But Francesco is a young man, he couldn't have made Elaine Carnet pregnant way back in nineteen forty-five or forty-six."

"Papa Pullini could have. Papa Pullini is a businessman and he was a businessman in nineteen forty-five too. He must have traveled. We know he speaks French, Bergen told us so. Maybe he went to Paris, strayed into a nightclub, saw the beautiful singer, bought her a bunch of roses, started a romance."

'So she waits thirty years and revenges herself on Papa Pullini's son, is that what you're saying?"

Grijpstra got up and walked over to the window.

"Very weak," de Gier said softly. "Now what if Bergen was the wicked father? Or the baboon? They're the right age."

Grijpstra turned around. "I know. But the commissaris went to Milano. I thought of Bergen too, but why would she pick him as a business partner? And the same goes for the baboon. She worked with both men for many years. Why would she work with a man, and allow him to share her profits, if she had every reason to despise that man?

And where do the eighty thousand guilders fit in? And the twenty thousand that the baboon borrowed and returned? That money does exist. Did you count the money Gabrielle showed to you, Cardozo?"

"Yes, adjutant. There were one hundred thousand guilder notes, eighty new, twenty slightly used."

Grijpstra's index finger came up. "See, sergeant? The money was there. Francesco took the lot and rushed out of the house. He counted the money in his hotel and found more than he expected. He phoned Gabrielle. She told him that she had removed his fingerprints and that he was safe but that he should return the money to her. She probably promised to pay him the eighty later, officially, out of the firm's account—she could make that promise for she inherits the firm, Bergen only owns a quarter of it, she could override all his decisions I am sure Francesco would have given the twenty back anyway I don't think he's a robber, he just wanted what was due him."

"And he killed Elaine in anger," de Gier said slowly. "That'll help him in court, if he confesses. He should come and see us and give himself up, that's why the commissaris didn't want us to make an arrest while he was away."

"Exactly."

"Adjutant?"

"Yes, Cardozo?"

"But Elaine was a bit of a bitch, wasn't she? She knew that her daughter was having an affair with Francesco and that Francesco was Gabrielle's half-brother. She could have stopped the affair, couldn't she?"

Grijpstra shrugged. "Perhaps, but Gabrielle might not have cared. I would say that Gabrielle's real feeling is for the baboon and that Francesco was something on the side, strong enough to protect him against us but still . . She jumped at you at the drop of a hat, didn't she? She probably has lots of sex, here, there, and everywhere."

Cardozo blushed.

De Gier got up too and joined Grijpstra at the window. "I don't know, Grijpstra. Elaine had an affair with the baboon and he got himself out of it, even at the expense of losing his job. Next thing we know is that Gabrielle dives into his bed. Elaine may have known. There may have been a terrific scene between mother and daughter, which would explain the wedding ring on the floor too. Gabrielle kills her mother. That way she has the business and the baboon and is free forever after.''

"And who was smoking the cigars that evening?"

De Gier walked back to his desk. "True. It would be nice if we could prove that angle, wouldn't it?"

"Here," Grijpstra said.

They all looked at the long narrow tin of cigars the adjutant had placed on de Gier's desk. "Signorinas, made in Brazil. I found this tin late last night, had to wake up my cousin who owns a tobacco store. Expensive cigars for successful businessmen, my cousin doesn't sell too many of them. He says they are really excellent cigars. Maybe he is right, I tried one and they taste rather perfumed. Cardozo can take the tin and check the cigar counter in the Pulitzer Hotel and all the tobacconists around it. He should be able to come up with a statement that says that a man of Francesco's description bought the cigars on the evening of Mrs. Carnet's death. The statement won't mean too much in court, but it'll mean something. At least we'll be able to prove that Francesco was lying when he said that he didn't visit Elaine Carnet on the evening of her death.''

Cardozo took the tin and left.

"Anything else we can do while the commissaris is away?"

Grijpstra grinned. "Sure. We can go to the snack bar around the corner and drink some real coffee and enjoy a quiet twenty minutes. And then we might go and visit the baboon again."

"Why?"

"Why not? He's an interesting man, isn't he?"

"O.K. And Bergen?"

"He's having more tests this morning, but I think we should contact him later in the day. They've all been lying, of course, hiding facts. Everybody has been hoping that we'll give up and consider the easiest way out.''

De Gier nodded. "Write it off as an accident. Good, we'll go and shake them, but I don't think it's necessary. The commissaris is bound to come up with something conclusive."

"I think I'll become a mercenary," de Gier said a little later in the snack bar. He held up the paper and showed Grijpstra a photograph of a fat, jolly black man in a general's uniform. "This guy has killed a few thousand people in his country, why don't we go and get him? Why must we go after a tiny little Italian who doesn't really mean any harm?"

Grijpstra choked on a meat roll. De Gier waited.

"The Italian is here," Grijpstra said finally, when he had finished coughing.

"We could go there, couldn't we?"

"I am here too."

"And if you were there?"

Grijpstra took the paper and looked at the photograph. The fat general was still smiling. Grijpstra stuffed the rest of the meat roll into his mouth. He chewed for another minute.

"Well?"

"I would kill him," Grijpstra said and wiped his mouth. "It would be fun. We could think it out carefully, make it look like an accident, set up some sort of a trap. The commissaris would like that too. He could sit in his bath and build a trap out of subtleties, do it step by step, each step a little more slithery than the one before, create a safety system for the general's protection, for instance, but the system suddenly malfunctions and poof!"

Grijpstra's fingertip tapped the general's forehead. They walked to the counter together. Grijpstra stepped back so that de Gier could pay.

"Yes," de Gier said, "the commissaris would like that."

18

"Very very sorry," Pullini said. "I will buy new truck for Eraldo. That old truck, he has bad brakes. I warn him many times but Eraldo, he keeps driving truck. Eraldo, he says you broke your cane, yes?"

The commissaris felt in his pocket. He put the handle on the table. Pullini picked it up. He shook his head in silent consternation.

"Nice handle, beautiful handle. Maybe I can get you a new cane. Really very sorry. Eraldo, he could have hit you, yes? Fortunately he turned wheel just in time, but say he had not, then what would happen? Commissaire de la police municipale d'Amsterdam dead in Sesto San Giovanni. Accident, of course. Constable here, he says accident. Eraldo, he says accident. Many witnesses say accident. But you, you dead commissaire."

The commissaris took off his glasses and began to polish them. His eyes twinkled. The wine had been excellent, so had the meal. Proper gourmet food, exquisitely cooked. A lovely salad. Even the ice cream had been outstanding, and the service could be called personal, very personal. Renata had served every dish and had hovered around the table in between courses, managing to be both inconspicuous and lovely.

He couldn't argue about Pullini's good taste as he couldn't have argued with Eraldo's little green pickup that had missed him but had taken his cane and crushed it. Eraldo was, indeed, a good driver. Pullini's chauffeur had taken his chances, another fraction of an inch and the commissaris would have been caught by the sleeve, whirled around, and smashed into the cobblestones. As it was he had fallen, but the truck, in spite of its alleged absence of brakes, had stopped a few hundred feet down the road and come back to pick him up. Eraldo had been most apologetic and solicitous. He had brushed the commissaris's jacket and helped him into the truck's cabin and delivered him at the Ristorante Pullini. A good show.

"Now," Pullini said, rubbing his wide hands, "we have eaten and now we talk. Something I understand now. Francesco, he has been silly, Elaine, she has been also silly. Sillier, for now she is dead."

"Did you speak to your son this afternoon?"

"Oh, yes." Pullini smiled benignly. Yes, he had finally got through to Amsterdam. Francesco was quite sure that the police suspected him of having pushed Mrs. Carnet down the stairs, and he was also quite sure that he was caught. His passport had already been taken away, soon he might be in jail.

"And did he kill Mrs. Carnet?"

Pullini's right hand balled up and began to turn. Well, perhaps something did happen. But it was an accident, of course. There had been a scene, a terrible scene. Francesco was very upset, also on the telephone. Perhaps Papa Pullini should have told his son about the romantic adventure so long ago, and so far away, all the way to Paris.

Pullini poured more wine, barola, a rich wine. He spilled a little, and Renata's lithe body came between them to sprinkle salt on the stain. Pullini was talking volubly. He had been in Paris at the time to buy luxuries that could be sold to the American officers in Milano. It had been a good time, but difficult, for he had to learn so much. Fortunately some of the American officers had spoken Italian. That had been a help, but even so. He was gesturing wildly. Even so, a struggle, yes. But he had earned the capital necessary to buy his furniture business. And he had enjoyed himself in Paris.

"Where you met Elaine Carnet?"

"Oh, yes, surely."

"But you didn't marry her. Why not, Mr. Pullini?"

Amazement spread over Pullini's gleaming cheeks. Marry a nightclub singer? A foreigner? When he had just invested his entire capital in a furniture factory? He needed connections in those days. He needed textiles to upholster his furniture, didn't he? And the young lady he married was the daughter of a textile manufacturer.

"So Francesco thinks we may put him in jail?" The commissaris asked the question gently, patting his lips with the snow-white napkin that Renata had just handed him.

He had taken a few seconds to admire Renata. She had noticed his admiration and the raven-black eyes had flashed. Pullini had noticed too. He was grinning.

"You like her, yes?"

"Beautiful," the commissaris agreed.

"Renata, she sleeps upstairs. Perhaps we can have a small glass with her later, yes? Restaurant, he close soon."

"Jail," the commissaris reminded his host.

Pullini laughed. Yes. Francesco is such a dear boy, he imagines things. Pullini suddenly looked sad. He launched into another monologue. Police officers in Italy are very badly paid, so thoughtless of the government, no doubt it was the same in Holland. Police officers are hard-working officials, but who thinks of them as they risk their lives in the middle of the night chasing the bad men? Or nearly get run over by a truck in a foreign country? So many police officers think of themselves sometimes and arrange a little this or that. Pullini's balled hand was turning again as if it wanted to bore a hole into a wall. Police officers know many people. Perhaps some of those people would be connected with the furniture trade. It might be possible that a certain commissaire would like to be connected with a certain furniture business, on a monthly basis. Or yearly. Part of the profits. A little more wine, perhaps?

"Yes," the commissaris said and smiled benevolently. Another glass of barola, a majestic wine.

"So?" Pullini asked.

"No, sir. Perhaps Italian police officers are badly paid but the Dutch police cannot complain. The salaries are quite adequate. And they are not so interested in business; business has to do with buying and selling and distribution and so on, a different kettle of fish from what Dutch police officers are used to doing for a living, Monsieur Pullini, very different."

Pullini wiped his face. His eyes, slightly bloodshot, became calm. He picked up his glass but it was empty, and Renata moved closer. He waved her away.

"Your leg," Pullini said quietly, "it hurts, yes?"

"Yes, I suffer from rheumatism."

Ah. Pullini's eyes gleamed again. He knew all about rheumatism. His mother, old Mrs. Pullini, bless her soul, also suffered from rheumatism, but she had gone to the mountains and there, no more pain. She was dead now but her last years were peaceful years. No pain, no pain at all. The mountain air is clean and quiet and known to cure many ailments. And so it happened that he, Pullini, had a little chalet for sale, a beautiful chalet. The price, for a friend, would be very reasonable, almost nothing in fact, maybe even nothing at all. A token payment so that the deed could be passed and registered in the friend's name.

The commissaris held up his glass and Renata filled it.

The raven-black eyes flashed, the hips swung smoothly, the narrow skirt split and there was a glimmer of a firm white thigh.

"Maybe," Pullini said quietly, "maybe we go upstairs now and we talk about chalet, yes?"

But the commissaris was shaking his head. "Non."

Pullini breathed out. The breath took a number of seconds and seemed to take all the air out of his body. He sank back in his chair. When he spoke again his voice was low and precise.

"Commissaire, what can you prove against my son?"

The commissaris put his glass down. "Enough, sir.

There are statements by witnesses. Your son has lied to us and we can prove that he lied. My detectives are working now but we don't really need any more proof. The judge will convict your son."

Pullini looked at Renata. He was smiling helplessly.

She held up the bottle and he nodded.

"So, commissaire, why you not arrest my son? My son, he is in hotel, yes? Not in jail."

"Your son must confess, sir. He must come and see us and tell us what he did, how he did it, and exactly why he did it. He must describe everything that happened."

"Why, commissaire?"

"It will be better. Your son did not murder Elaine Carnet, he only killed her. He didn't plan her death. He got angry and he pushed, that's all."

Pullini's heavy body had straightened up. He was staring at his opponent. His hand pressed and pushed the table-cloth.

"Yes? So all right, Francesco, he confesses, then judge, he sends Francesco to jail. How long?"

"Not so long."

"Years?"

"Months. There are extenuating circumstances. Our charges will be modest. But he must come to us, he must tell us what he did."

A cold calculating light had crept into Pullini's eyes. "So he confesses, so very easy for police municipale d'Amsterdam, not so? Police, she maybe know nothing, she maybe guesses, and here stupid Italian boy, he walks right up and he says, 'Me, I guilty, please take me.' "

"No, we know what he did. If he doesn't come we will have to take him from his hotel. The case will be much worse."

Pullini's mouth tried to sneer but the expression trembled away before it had a chance to form itself clearly. The sneer became a joyless smile that did little more than show Pullini's expensive teeth.

"You trap me, yes? Me, I tell you that Francesco, he pushes Elaine. I know because Francesco, he tell me. He also tell me about the eighty thousand guilders. He already confesses, to accident and to stealing from his father. I knew about the stealing, not how much, but that not important. His life different to mine, for Francesco everything easy from beginning, too easy. Maybe better to start off with baby birds and one peacock. Well . . ."

His hands rose slowly from the tablecloth, then dropped from their own weight. "You trap me, yes. But how do you know all this? How do you know Gabrielle is Pullini's daughter?"

Once his cleverness had left him Pullini's face changed strangely, perhaps to its truest form. The powerful jaws smoothed into round, innocent lines that continued so that they held the bald skull too, and the eyes, bereft of their cunning glint, became bland and almost transparent.

The commissaris's small thin hand was pointing, and Pullini turned around to see what he was pointing to. A portrait of a young woman singing, the woman's smooth arm resting on the top of an upright piano.

"Elaine," Pullini said. "Yes, that is Elaine. *Was* Elaine, thirty years ago in Paris. But she must be changed in thirty years, Francesco, he did not know her like that. You, you never knew her. How do you know that is Elaine? You guessing again, yes?"

"There is another copy of that portrait." The commissaris told Pullini where he had seen it.

Pullini nodded. "Two portraits, eh? Elaine, she keep one, and she send me one. In parcel; no letter, no nothing. Just portrait. I like it and I hang it here, in my restaurant where I eat every day. Me, I don't go home much. But no proof for you, commissaire. You, you do not know that Elaine, she sends portrait to me. You only see portrait when you come here."

"It is proof now," the commissaris said, holding up his glass. Renata brought a new bottle of barola. The other guests had left; the two men had the restaurant and the woman to themselves. Renata locked the door and switched off most of the lights. There was no further conversation until Renata opened the door and the two men entered the narrow street and walked the few blocks to the hotel, arms around each other's shoulders, swaying in unison.

"Tomorrow you go, yes?"

"Yes."

"Me, I go with you. What time your plane he leaves?"

"At ten in the morning."

"Good, we breakfast together, yes?"

"Yes."

Barola is a good wine. It seeps away both aggression and resistance. Their embrace was quiet and dignified.

"Me, I am sorry about Eraldo's truck. But I tried, yes? Eraldo, he good driver. When he is told to miss, he miss."

"Yes," the commissaris said.

"Tomorrow I buy you new cane. I have handle. Same handle, new cane."

"Yes."

They peered into each other's face. A half-moon had dipped the small quiet square into an eerie haze of soft white light that encircled the vast dark mass of a widely branched oak, a comforting central ornament caressing the cobblestones with its deep purple, almost imperceptibly moving shadows. The commissaris watched Pullini's squat body turn ponderously. Pullini could still walk on his own, but he had to find his way slowly in the square's silence, stopping every few steps to make sure of his direction. Three identical little Fiats, pushing their noses into the pavement, provided support in turn until Pullini, with a final lunge of great deliberation, located the gaping dark mouth of the small alley that would take him back to his restaurant and Renata's comforts.

The commissaris shook his head and began to walk to the hotel door. He noted, to his surprise, that he had sobered up again and that he wasn't even tired. It seemed a pity to withdraw from the square's tranquillity and he turned back, feeling the polished surfaces of the cobblestones through the thin soles of his shoes. He rested for a while against the oak's trunk until he began to feel cold and pushed himself free reluctantly.

The case was solved. He had been very sly, basing his

attack on shaky proofs and a web of deductions that fitted but could be shaken loose by any lawyer for the defense. If he had given himself more time the proofs would have been substantiated sufficiently to stand up in court, but he had been pushing the case at breakneck speed. But Francesco would no doubt confess now and make further work unnecessary. The prosecution wouldn't be too hard on the suspect and the punishment would be mild. That, in a way, was a pleasant consequence of the method he had applied.

But why had he been in such an infernal hurry? Yes. His small head nodded firmly at the hotel door's polished brass knob. There was more to the case, and he had better get back to see how the pus, festering out of the wound slashed by Pullini when he refused to marry Elaine, was spreading. Perhaps he should have had the other actors, the baboon, Bergen, and Gabrielle, and Francesco too, locked up. But it isn't the task of the police to lock up citizens who are potentially dangerous to each other. Jail space is limited and reserved for those who have translated their faulty thinking into wrong acts. He had better get back quickly. But he would have to wait for the morning plane. And meanwhile he could have another bath. When nothing can be done it is not a bad idea to do nothing. The profundity of the thought helped him up the hotel's stairs.

19

When Grijpstra turned the key of the Volkswagen in the garage of headquarters, a voice grated from a loudspeaker attached to the roof directly above the car.

"Adjutant Grijpstra."

"No," Grijpstra said, but he got out and trotted obediently to the telephone that the garage's sergeant was holding up for him.

"Yes?"

"A message came in for your brigade, adjutant," a radio room constable said. "A certain Dr. Havink called, about a Mr. Bergen. Dr. Havink didn't ask for you in particular, but he mentioned Mr. Bergen, and one of the detectives told me that he had read the name in the Carnet case file."

"Yes, yes, very good of you, thank you, constable. What was the message?"

"This Mr. Bergen has disappeared or something. I didn't really catch on, but I've got Dr. Havink's number here. Would you call him please, adjutant?"

"Yes." Grijpstra wrote the number down, waved at de Gier, and dialed. De Gier picked up the garage's second phone and pressed a button.

"Dr. Havink? CID here. I believe you called just now."

The doctor's voice was quiet, noncommittal. "Yes. I am

concerned about a patient, a Mr. Bergen, Mr. Frans Bergen. Does that name mean anything to you?''

"It does, doctor."

"Good, or bad perhaps, I wouldn't know. The point is that Mr. Bergen had a nervous breakdown in my office this morning and left before I had a chance to stop him. According to my nurse, the patient was talking to himself and kept on mentioning the words 'police' and 'killing.' Would you like to come to my office or can I explain over the telephone?''

"You say Mr. Bergen has left, doctor? Did he say where he was going?''

"He left and didn't say where he was going, and he appeared to be very upset. My nurse says that the patient kept on patting his pocket and that it's possible that he was carrying a firearm.''

"Go on, doctor."

The doctor's report was clear. Bergen had arrived that morning at eight-thirty for his final test. The test was designed to determine whether or not the patient's skull held a tumor. The patient's blood had been colored and the blood's flow through the brain had been checked. The result was negative, no tumor. The patient had been asked to wait in a small room adjoining the doctor's study. The door between the two rooms was ajar so that Bergen could see what the doctor was doing. Dr. Havink had been looking at the results of another test, nothing to do with Bergen. The results of that particular test had been positive, a case of brain cancer in an advanced state. While Bergen waited, Dr. Havink had telephoned a colleague to discuss the other patient's test.

"Ah," Grijpstra said. "I see, and Mr. Bergen could hear what you were saying on the telephone."

"Yes, most unfortunate, I should have made sure that the door was closed. It usually is, but it wasn't this morning.''

"Go on, doctor, what did you tell your colleague?''

Dr. Havink's meticulous voice described the course of events. He had told his colleague that the test's results were of such a definite nature that he didn't think that the patient had more than a week to live and that an operation would be useless. The conversation had taken about five minutes, and during that time Bergen must have left the small waiting room and gone back to the main waiting room, where, according to the nurse, he began to pace about and talk to himself in a loud voice.

"And pat his pocket," Grijpstra said.

Yes, and pat his pocket. Mr. Bergen talked about the police, about money, and about killing. Then he left. The nurse tried to stop him but he pushed her aside. And so Dr. Havink called the police.

"I see, I see. So we may assume that Mr. Bergen understood that your verdict referred to him. He wasn't aware that you were talking about another patient."

"Yes. I am sorry about this. It's an occurrence that has never happened before but it could have, obviously, for it has happened now. My arrangement here is faulty. The door between my office and the little waiting room should have been closed, and I should have told Mr. Bergen that I would be discussing his case with him in a minute but that I had to take care of something else first. The whole thing is pathetic, really. There is nothing the matter with Mr. Bergen. We did three tests on him and they were all negative, although the X-ray did show a small calcification, but this is nothing unusual. Still, we continue checking in such a case, routine, simple routine. All Mr. Bergen has is a facial nerve infection that will cure itself; his face should have some movement again soon, in a few days, I would say. But I didn't have a chance to tell him."

Grijpstra sighed and looked at de Gier. De Gier was shaking his head.

"Yes, doctor. Thank you for letting us know. We'll see if we can find Mr. Bergen. Do you happen to recall what he was wearing?"

"A dark suit, crumpled as if he had slept in it, no tie, open shirt. He hadn't shaved."

"Thank you."

De Gier had put his telephone down and was standing

next to the adjutant. "An alert, don't you think? A general alert. Bergen will be running around somewhere. He wouldn't have gone home or to his office, but I'll check."

Bergen's home phone didn't answer. A secretary at his office said he wasn't there. "Miss Gabrielle Carnet?" Gabrielle hadn't arrived yet. De Gier telephoned the Carnet house. No answer.

"O.K., an alert, for what it's worth. The patrol cars never see very much, their windows are all steamed up."

Grijpstra telephoned the radio room. He described Bergen and added that the suspect was in a state of mental breakdown and probably armed. When he put the phone down he was smiling.

"What?"

Grijpstra prodded de Gier's stomach. "Crazy situation, don't you think? As the commissaris said, there is nothing wrong with the man, but Bergen has imagined himself into a terminal position, a good-bye maybe, or a complete breakdown that he hopes will leave him senseless. He must have slipped a pistol into his pocket before he went to Dr. Havink's clinic this morning. A pistol is a very violent instrument. He could have bought sleeping pills—he has a house of his own and a bed."

De Gier was scratching his bottom. "Sleeping pills are never very dramatic."

"Quite." Grijpstra was still smiling.

"But what's so funny?"

"Don't you see? The fellow has made all the mistakes he could make. He gets a letter from the bank that must be negotiable in some way. Banks always threaten, but if you owe them enough their threats don't stick; they can't afford to break your business, for if they do you can't pay them. But Bergen insists that his business is finished. His wife sends him a lawyer's letter and he cracks up. Can't he sit down and figure out whether he really wants her? If he doesn't want her there's no problem, he can sell his house and find a good apartment somewhere, or even a few good rooms. With his money he can find a woman to go with the rooms and state his terms. But if he really wants his wife back, well, he can find her and talk to her, can't he? There may still be an opening for an approach, but no, he chooses to rush around and mess up his house and ruin one of his cars and burn holes in the carpet."

"Very funny, what else?"

"This paralysis, of course. You heard what Dr. Havink said. It's a minor affliction, a nothing. It will go away if he has the patience to wait a few days. But he doesn't even have the patience to wait for the doctor to come out of his office, for he has already convinced himself that he is suffering from brain cancer and has a week to live and he has rushed out into the street, screaming."

"Hilarious. And now we have him wandering around, a raving lunatic with a deadly weapon. Does he have a car with him?"

"Probably. We saw a new Volvo in his driveway last night."

"So he may be anywhere by now."

The loudspeaker in the garage's ceiling croaked again. "Adjutant Grijpstra."

"Oh, for God's sake!" But the adjutant turned and marched back to the phone.

The radio room constable apologized. "We know you're busy, adjutant, but the commissaris isn't here and the inspector is out on an urgent call and I can't raise him. We have a call from a patrol They were asked to go to an address on the Amsteldijk, Number One-seven-two. Neighbors heard a shot in the top apartment, first an angry male voice, then a shot. The constables broke the apartment's door and found blood on the floor but no one is there. The apartment belongs to a Mr Vleuten. I have been trying to find Adjutant Geurts, he's probably out having coffee somewhere. Shall I ask him to go to the Amsteldijk when he comes in?"

"No, we'll go."

"Siren?" de Gier asked.

"No."

Grijpstra was sitting behind the wheel, the engine idling. "Hospitals?" de Gier said. "The baboon is wounded,

He isn't the sort of man to wander around. He has a car, perhaps he can still drive it."

"University Hospital." Grijpstra said. "That's where I would go if I lived on the Amsteldijk and got shot. Maybe the Wilhelmina is closer but you get stuck in traffic. Let's have that siren."

The small car dug itself into the heavy morning traffic, howling furiously. A large white Uzzi motorcycle appeared, and de Gier shouted at the constable riding it.

"University Hospital, lead the way."

The constable saluted. The motorcycle's siren joined in, and the Uzzi reared and shot away with the Volkswagen trailing its gleaming suave form while cars stopped and bicycles fled to the pavement.

"Easy," de Gier shouted as the Volkswagen's fender ground past a streetcar's bumper, but Grijpstra didn't react. He sat hunched behind the wheel, twisting it to make the car follow the motorcycle. The car's engine whined and the sirens howled on gleefully.

The dented Volkswagen swung into the hospital's parking lot and came to rest next to the baboon's Rolls-Royce, shining in splendid isolation between a row of mud-spattered compacts. The motorcycle cop waved and rode off as Grijpstra and de Gier clambered out of the car and began to run toward the emergency entrance. A nurse directed them, and they found the victim sitting on a plastic chair in a small white room. Gabrielle sat on the bed, swinging her legs.

"Very good," the baboon said, looking at his watch. "I got shot an hour ago and here you are already. The deadly detectives."

Grijpstra grinned.

"But I'm all right," the baboon said, and he pointed at his bandage. The bandage hid his short neck and his left ear. "A minor wound. If Gabrielle hadn't insisted I would have used a Band-Aid."

"And he would have bled to death, the doctor said so."

"And I would have bled to death."

"Who?" de Gier asked.

The baboon was rolling a cigarette.

"Who?"

The baboon looked up. "A bad man. I won't tell you. He is in enough trouble now without your adding to it."

"Oh," Gabrielle said, "you are such a *fool*, baboon. Sometimes you overdo it, you know. If you don't tell them I will."

"Who?" De Gier's voice hadn't changed. He felt very patient.

"Bergen, of course. He came running into the apartment waving a gun and holding his face. He was such a *mess*."

"But why the aggression? What does Mr. Bergen have against the baboon?"

"Gabrielle being with me didn't help much," the baboon said and felt his bandage. "This scratch hurts, you know. Do you know that the cow's skeleton saved me?" The baboon began to laugh, a pleasant rumbly laugh. "You should have been there. Gabrielle didn't have any clothes on and all I had was a towel, and Bergen kept standing there, shouting away. I pressed the button and the cow came out of the cupboard, directly in his path, so he had to jump aside and he couldn't aim, but the bullet did make contact and I fell, so he probably thought he had got me and ran. And meanwhile the cow had made its full circle and gone back into the cupboard. And Gabrielle was holding her breasts and screaming." The baboon was wiping his eyes.

"Yes," Gabrielle said, "very funny. And I am to blame, of course. Francesco phoned last night and foulmouthed me too. As if it's my fault that I'm his half-sister. He has forgotten that I have been helping him, but I won't help anybody anymore."

"So will you make a statement now, Miss Carnet?"

"About what?"

"That Mr. Pullini pushed your mother down the stairs. We do have some sort of a witness's statement but it isn't enough."

"Anything," Gabrielle said, "anything you like. I'm tired of this tangle. That idiot Bergen thinks he can be jealous too, and that he can use me. *Nobody* can use me.'' Her voice no longer purred and her eyes seemed to have shrunk and were glittering with fury. De Gier took his chance.

"There was something between you and Mr. Bergen, Miss Carnet?"

"Something? What is something? We have been on business trips together and maybe we had a little too much to drink and maybe I let him get away with being such a powerful male. That was a long time ago, a year maybe. But he fussed. He fussed so much that his wife heard about it and finally left him."

"He thought he loved you?"

"Love." Her eyes narrowed and her lips pouted.

"You didn't love him?"

"Of course not."

The baboon had gotten up and was walking to the door.

"Are you leaving, Mr. Vleuten?"

"I may as well. I was waiting for the nurse to come back but it seems she won't. I have things to do. So have you, I imagine."

"We'll have to find Mr. Bergen."

The baboon stopped near the door. "Where?"

"Exactly. Where could he be?"

The baboon turned and leaned against the wall. "A good question. Have you seen him recently? I was wondering what brought on this sudden attack? He was shouting a lot but I didn't understand him."

Grijpstra explained.

"Cancer?"

"He thinks he has cancer, that he has a week to live."

The baboon fingered his bandage. "I see. So I became the enemy. I've been the enemy before, when he thought I would marry Elaine and take the business away from him. But I didn't and I thought that obstacle was removed. Maybe it wasn't, maybe he kept on blaming me."

Grijpstra leant his bulk against the wall of the sterile little room and smoked peacefully. "For taking Miss Carnet away?"

"Possibly. But there were other reasons. He was man-ufacturing them, ever since we met, I think. Perhaps it started when I was bringing in a lot of orders."

"Jealousy?"

The baboon was still stroking the bandage. "More than that, I think. Bergen never felt very secure. He didn't want to blame himself so he found me. The fact that he took a shot at me just now may prove that theory."

Grijpstra looked at the smoke crinkling out of his cigar. "You won, he lost. Quite."

"Not quite. Unless you can define what constitutes the ideas 'to win' and 'to lose.' " The baboon's eyes were twinkling.

"Yes, Mr. Vleuten?"

"You should have seen that damned cow. Zooming at him and then turning and disappearing again. I would never have thought that the thing would protect me. I had con-structed it for the absolute opposite. It was supposed to frighten me."

"Oh, you're so *crazy*." Gabrielle had snuggled into the baboon's arm. She was looking into his face, touching his cheek gently with her pointed nails.

"I'm not so crazy, " the baboon said. "I'm just trying to do things from a different angle. Only trying. It's hard to go against the flow, maybe it's impossible. What hap-pened this morning rather underlines that, doesn't it? I cre-ate an object of fear, maybe ridiculous to others but really fearsome to me, and it saves my life. But I won't give in."

"Mr. Bergen," de Gier said firmly, "we've got to find him. Do you have any idea where he is, baboon?"

"Bergen is under great stress. He is wandering around," Grijpstra added. "You must have gotten to know the man fairly well. Can you think of any place Bergen would go if he thought he was in real trouble?"

The baboon was looking out the window. "Yes," he said slowly, "yes, perhaps I know."

"Where?"

"He surprised me once. I always thought the man had no soul, you know, that he was only concerned with selling furniture. But we came back from a trip once, in his car, and we were late, we had been speeding, for he wanted to be home in time for dinner. When we got near the city it was after seven o'clock and he said his wife wouldn't have waited for him and he turned the car off the highway. We went to a little village on the river and had dinner there and some brandy afterward, and later we went for a walk."

"He went to that village on purpose? You didn't just happen to find it on your way?"

"No, he knew the place, he had been there before. He told me that his father used to take him to the village sometimes and that they would always have dinner in that little pub and then go for a walk. We ended up in a small cemetery, very old, with moss-covered stones, and we walked about. He seemed very peaceful that evening. I had never seen him like that before."

"What's the name of the village?"

"Nes. I can take you there. Nes on the Amstel. Only a few houses and a church and the pub. We had to cross the river in a little ferry to get to it."

De Gier had opened the door. "Shall I get the water police?" he asked Grijpstra.

"No. Why don't you go with the baboon and Miss Carnet can come with me. I'll follow the Rolls. Nes is only about a quarter of an hour from here. Perhaps we'll still be in time. If we get assistance we'll delay ourselves unnecessarily. What sort of handgun did Bergen use, baboon?"

"A revolver."

"He only took one shot at you?"

"Yes."

"So he has five bullets left." Grijpstra groaned and sighed simultaneously.

"A nice little job. Shall we go?"

20

It took awhile before Grijpstra had time to talk to Gabrielle. He was busy with his radio while the Volkswagen, gray and inconspicuous, followed the regal backside of the Rolls along the road clinging to the river. The radio room had connected him with the commissaris, and their conversation was linking their separate adventures.

"Very well, sir, so Papa Pullini is now at the hotel talking to his son?" Grijpstra looked at the microphone. He hadn't released the button yet, so the commissaris couldn't reply. "And you expect Francesco to come in sometime today to make his peace with us?"

The button sprang back and the commissaris's soft voice mixed with the high-pitched sound of the car's engine and the squeak of its battered shock absorbers.

"Yes, adjutant, that side of the case should be fixed. Cardozo will be here to take their statement, I think he'll be able to follow Francesco's English. Cardozo tells me that he's found the tobacconist that sold the cigars Francesco smoked when he visited Mrs. Carnet. I think I'll be joining you and the sergeant presently, but I'll probably arrive too late. You have almost reached Nes, you say?"

"Almost, sir, I can see the ferry sign, it should be just

around the corner, and the village should be a few hundred yards farther down.''

"Right. I'll be there as soon as I can. Out.''

Grijpstra replaced the microphone and turned to Gabrielle. ''You've had an exciting morning, Miss Carnet.''

"It's still going on.'' She had used the time to adjust her make-up and comb her hair and seemed to have recovered some of her composure. ''A real crisis, isn't it? I never expected Bergen to lose himself so completely. He was a raving maniac when he attacked the baboon. I'd gone into the bathroom when the bell rang, but when I heard the shot . . .''

Grijpstra mused. He remembered the young woman who had shot her husband. It had happened a few weeks before, early in the morning. Just after nine, he and de Gier had just gone out on their patrol and were waiting at the first traffic light. The couple was about to get divorced and the man had been ready to go to work when his wife shot him in the face, point-blank, with no more than a foot between the pistol's muzzle and the man's forehead. She had telephoned the police herself, and the detectives had arrived within a matter of minutes. The woman was crying when de Gier took the weapon out of her hand. A hopeless case. The couple had a little son, four years old, wandering about the apartment. Father dead, mother in jail. They had taken the boy to the crisis center; he hadn't dared to check what they had done with him. The crisis center wasn't a good place to check with, its staff was continuously overworked. He hoped that the center had found good foster parents and that the boy wasn't being shifted around.

Gabrielle was talking and he forced himself to listen.

"Was he really saved by that crazy contraption, miss?''

Gabrielle kept her eyes on the Rolls's rear bumper. "Yes, he must have been. The crazy skeleton, I knew it was there. He never showed it to me but I pressed the cupboard's button once, thinking it was a light switch, and I became hysterical when the horror lunged out at me. Crazy, like the baboon himself. Just look at that car. There's hardly any money, between his mortgage payments on his house and the rents he is collecting and he has to pay for the upkeep, there are always lots of repairs. He is living on a few hundred guilders a month, but if he takes me out he won't let me pay and we go to a sandwich bar somewhere and we sit in the front row of the cinema. But he runs a car like that. When he can't afford to pay for gas he takes the streetcar; often he walks.''

''Doesn't he sell boats?''

She shrugged. ''There isn't much profit in that, either. I wish he'd come back and work for us, he could have a good income and he'd be worth it too.''

The Rolls had parked near the ruins of a mill, and the baboon and de Gier were walking to a small brick building almost hidden under a patched thatch roof. Grijpstra squeezed the Volkswagen between the Rolls and a tree.

A hunchbacked man behind the bar was pumping four beers and listening to de Gier at the same time.

''Yes,'' he said, deftly wiping the beer's foam into the counter's small sink, ''he was here. About an hour ago. Had a few beers and drank them through a straw. First time I've ever seen beer drunk through a straw.''

''Was he talking to himself?''

''No. He was quiet. I've seen him here before. A well-behaved gentleman, but he looked somewhat scruffy today. Out on a binge, is he?''

''Yes. Where would he be now?''

''Should I tell you?''

De Gier produced his police card, and the man took a pair of horn-rimmed spectacles from a drawer. He studied the card and tugged on the end of his scraggly mustache. ''Police, hmm. Never see police here except the local constable and he's my brother. Nice job if you can avoid the poachers but he can do it. You'll be different, I suppose.''

Grijpstra drank his beer and the hunchback left the bar and peered through a side window. ''That's his car, I think, so he can't be far. Seems he wanted to hide it, you can't see it from the road.''

The baboon came to life at his end of the bar. ''There's a cemetery close by, I remember. Where is it again, not far, is it?"

"Out the front door, turn right, first path on your right again, and you'll walk straight into it."

De Gier paid and they left the pub, but Grijpstra paused at the door. "It would be better if you stayed here, miss."

"No."

"Stay here," the baboon said. Gabrielle took a deep breath, but the men were out on the dike and the door had closed in her face.

The sun hung under a ragged edge of heavy clouds and its filtered light seemed to deepen the green of the grasslands all around them. A herd of spotted, light-colored cows was grazing close to the fence and a flock of unusually neat-looking sheep was moving away on the other side of the path.

"An experimental state farm," the baboon said. "I remember Bergen telling me about it. They have imported types of cattle here, special breeds. Bergen seemed to know all about the farm. I remember because he had never expressed any interest in anything that wasn't furniture. He was a different man out here."

A falcon hung above the field, whizzing its wings, its stiff pure white tailfeathers sticking out like a miniature fan.

The baboon pointed. "The cemetery. There's no cover here, he'll be able to see us coming."

Cartridges clicked into the chambers of the policemen's pistols. De Gier had taken the lead, sprinting toward a high gravestone so old that its writing had been eaten away by the weather and overgrown by thick, bristly lichen. The first shot rang out as he reached the stone, and Grijpstra and the baboon dropped into the grass on the sides of the path.

"Bergen!" Grijpstra's booming voice reached into the depth of the soundless cemetery that stretched away from them, aloofly tolerating their intrusion.

"Bergen! Come out of there! We're here to help you. You have misunderstood Dr. Havink. There's nothing the

matter with you, Bergen. Come out and let us talk to you."
Grijpstra's voice, even with all the air in his lungs behind
it, sounded calm and reassuring, but the cows, pushing
each other behind a duckweed-covered ditch, mooed
mournfully and offset his message. Grijpstra gestured at the
baboon. The baboon pushed himself up.

"Down! Stay down there. You'll only be in our way and
you are wounded already. Get those cows to shut up."

The baboon crawled back and jumped across the ditch.
The cows were still jostling each other, trying to see what
was going on, and he grabbed the biggest one by the horns
and pushed. The cow didn't move. His attempts startled a
pair of peewits that flew up from behind a cluster of
swamp reeds, calling shrilly.

Grijpstra got up, ran, and dropped behind a tombstone
crowned by three miniature angels that had once played
trumpets but were now staring sadly at their broken arms.
The closest angel had lost both its nose and chin and weeds
were crawling up its chubby legs. Grijpstra peered around
the legs.

"Bergen! You're all right. You only have palsy, no tumor. You hear! No tumor. There has been a mistake. Bergen!"

The cows mooed again furiously, irritated by the baboon,
who was still shoving their leader.

"Palsy," Grijpstra shouted. "It will go away by it—"

There was another shot, this time aimed at de Gier, who
had left his gravestone and was without cover as he jumped
to the next. He dropped as the shot cracked, and the bullet
whistled away in the general direction of the cows.

"Fool!" Grijpstra roared and de Gier looked around,
waving a weed with small pink flowers that he had picked
from a spot where the stone had powdered away so that
nature could reassert itself. He was close enough to be able
to speak to Grijpstra in a normal voice.

"You know what this is?"

"Keep your cover."

"Thousand-guilder weed, Grijpstra, *Centaurium ery-
thraea*, one of the very few I know by its Latin name.

Fairly rare, I believe, but it grows near the streetcar stop and I took some to the city's botanical garden the other day. Amazing, don't you think? It grows all over the place here.''

"De Gier," Grijpstra said pleadingly, "he must be close. It's hard to hear where the shot came from. These stones echo, I think, but he must be over there."

"Where?"

"There, near that damned prick."

"Prick?"

Grijpstra was pointing at a heavily ornamented phallus, sprouting a poll of withered grass on its crumbling extremity. It was nearly six feet high and throned on a huge granite slab.

De Gier moved and drew another shot. They heard the bullet's dull impact where it hit the earth; a tufted reed sagged and broke with a snap as the tuft touched the ground.

"How many bullets left?" de Gier asked.

"One for the baboon, three for us, two left."

"Can I move again—we'll have to draw the other two—or do you want to sit here all day?"

Grijpstra picked up a rock and threw it at a patch of dandelions that brightened a complicated ruin of several tombs that had tumbled together. The revolver cracked again.

"Bergen! Stop making an ass of yourself. We won't charge you, just get out of there. You're safe. We want to help you."

"Let me be!" Bergen's voice was high-pitched, hysterical with fear and rage.

"No, you're being senseless."

Several cows mooed simultaneously. Grijpstra tried to move and slipped; his face fell into a patch of raw earth and he sat up, spitting out dirt. He saw de Gier take aim carefully, supporting his right arm with his left. The pistol's bark was sharp and was followed immediately by the heavier retort of the revolver.

"Got him," de Gier shouted, "in the arm. And he's out of bullets. Come on, Grijpstra."

They ran but Grijpstra stumbled, and de Gier stopped to help him. They reached Bergen in time to see him press the revolver against his temple. They were both shouting but the shot drowned their words. Bergen's head snapped to the side as if it had been hit by a sledgehammer, and his body tumbled against the phallus and slid down slowly until it rested on the grave's rubble. A small pile of cartridges had been stacked neatly into a cavity on the gravestone's surface.

De Gier took out his handkerchief and manipulated Bergen's revolver so that its chamber became detached. Its compartments were empty except for one. He closed the gun again and let the hand drop back.

"He just had enough time to slip in one more cartridge."

"Yes," Grijpstra said. "If I hadn't stumbled we would have got him in time. What a mess." He pointed at the blood seeping out of the corpse's head. It was trickling off the stone and mixing with another little stream pouring out of the man's arm. De Gier looked away. Grijpstra replaced his pistol into the holster on his belt and stretched. His back ached. It was very hot, and he thought of the cool pub on the dike and the cold beer that its polished barpump would splash into a polished glass.

When he turned he saw the commissaris running up the path, and he waved and shouted. The commissaris was supporting himself on a cane with a metal handle; he limped as he ran.

"Don't run, sir, it's all over."

The baboon had jumped back across the ditch and was moving through the fallen gravestones, waddling on his short legs. He reached the corpse at the same time as the commissaris.

"We tried to draw his fire, sir, and rushed him when we were sure the revolver was empty. De Gier had put a bullet in his right arm so we were doubly sure. But he had extra ammunition and he used his left hand."

The commissaris had knelt down and was examining Bergen's head. "Pity," he said quietly. "The skull must be badly damaged on the inside."

"He is quite dead, I think, sir."

"Oh, yes, that's clear. Dead. But there's something else, this case goes on, adjutant. Well, never mind. I'll think of something, but it's a pity about the skull."

21

De Gier's balcony door was open and the commissaris was sitting close to it, peering contentedly at his mug. De Gier faced him. He was coming to the end of his flute solo, a sixteenth-century drinking song, full of trills and quick runs and occasionally short intervals of almost mathematical precision. Grijpstra, his bristly mustache white with beer froth, was rubbing Tabriz's belly, smiling at the cat's droopy look of complete surrender. Cardozo was stretched out on the floor, his head resting on a small cushion propped on a stack of books.

De Gier lowered his flute. The commissaris inclined his head and applauded briefly. "Very good. Get him another beer, Grijpstra. Pity you couldn't bring your drums, it's been a long time since I heard you play together."

Grijpstra lumbered into the small kitchen and came back holding a fresh bottle. De Gier poured the beer, spilling a little. "I won't be able to play anymore, sir, the neighbors will be at my throat tomorrow."

Grijpstra had brought in another bottle but the commissaris shook his head. "I would like to, adjutant, but it's getting late, my wife'll be expecting me. Cardozo, how do you feel?"

Cardozo's eyes opened. He seemed to be thinking. The commissaris smiled. "Go back to sleep. I don't think either of us should drive."

It was past midnight. The lights in the park behind de Gier's apartment building had been switched on sometime before but the opaque white disks, spread among the willows and poplars, couldn't compete with the moon. The apartments around had gone to rest, and there were no sounds except an occasional rumbling from the boulevard on the other side of the building and the confused squeaking of a group of starlings that hadn't found the right tree for the night yet.

"We'll take a taxi. You can drive the Citroën to headquarters tomorrow, sergeant," the commissaris said firmly. "One of my colleagues got arrested for drunken driving last week. It reminded me how vulnerable we are."

"A brandy, sir?"

De Gier had struggled to his feet and was groping about behind his books. His hand came back holding a crystal decanter. Grijpstra's heavily lidded eyes were watching him.

"Just a nip, that would be very nice."

"A bad case," the commissaris said a little later. "But it's over and done with now. I didn't like it. There was too much pettiness in it."

Grijpstra stirred. There was a vague note of admonition in his voice. "We did have the baboon in it, sir."

The commissaris raised a finger. "Indeed. Its one ray of illumination, and he stayed true to type until the very end, you know . . ." He looked at the balcony. Cardozo had begun to snore softly, but his cushion slipped away, and he woke up and pushed it back.

The commissaris sipped his brandy thoughtfully. "You know, I thought he would give in and I didn't want him to give in. The baboon was drifting into a perfect, happy ending."

The commissaris giggled. "But he smartly stepped aside. Good for him. Happy endings are always so sad. I even thought so when I was a little boy and my mother would read fairy tales to me. I would cry when the princes married the princesses and settled down in the beautiful palaces. Whatever were they going to do forever after? Watch football or cartoons? Play cards? But the stories didn't tell, they didn't dare to, of course. Just suppose that the baboon would marry Gabrielle and move into that splendid home on the Mierisstraat with the sheik's tent upstairs. Just imagine.''

He put the brandy snifter down and brought out his handkerchief, wheezing into it energetically. "Our baboon, spending his nights on Gabrielle's couch while the young lady gradually sucks his soul away, wasting his days back in the furniture business, lodged safely in Bergen's office swiveling around on the president's chair, taking care of things."

'The Carnet Company will probably have to declare bankruptcy,'' Grijpstra said tonelessly, as if he were reading from a report.

"Oh, yes. Unless they have somebody on their staff who can take over, but that's rather doubtful. Or Gabrielle . . . no. I don't think she can do it. But the baboon can, easily. And he would be rich too. I don't think he would need more than a few years to get the company back on its feet and the bank would be sure to back him. Remember what Bergen told us? The bank liked the baboon.''

"Why do you think the baboon refused to become the company's president, sir?'' De Gier's voice was flat too.

"The *opposite,* dear boy.'' The commissaris said. "The *opposite.* Surely you've noticed.'' The commissaris blinked and took off his spectacles. "You *must* have noticed. You are leading an old man on. Or do you want me to confirm what you have already concluded yourself?''

"Please confirm it, sir.''

"What would the average man do if something frightened him? He would run away, wouldn't he? He would prefer to get away from whatever was causing him pain or anxiety. And if he could get hold of it he would try to kill it, or hide it somewhere deep in his mind so that he couldn't get close to it again, and so that it wouldn't be able to get at *him*. But the baboon recreated what he feared and kept his enemies in easily accessible places, on the wall of his apartment and in the cupboard. He set up his fear in such a way that it could charge him. You saw the rat's tail hanging out of that painting, de Gier You must have, for you are frightened of rats yourself Would you have a painting of a rat in here? And would you make it more gruesome by allowing the hellish fiend to let his tail hang out, right into the intimacy of your home?"

De Gier's face didn't move. His large eyes were staring at the commissaris.

"No. Don't answer me, you don't have to. We are discussing the baboon. He likes to do the opposite of wnat seems to be expected of him, and perhaps he evades the trap that way. He accepted neither Elaine's nor Gabrielle's offer. And yet he had worked for the Carnet ladies for ten years had been their chief salesman and their close friend, their lover even. They were offering him the whole caboodle, lock, stock, and barrel, with themselves thrown in. And Gabrielle's offer was even better than her mother's had been, for she is an attractive young woman."

Cardozo had woken and had pushed himself up against the bookcase.

"A most reasonable offer The intimate pleasures Gabrielle can dispense plus a firm that, if properly managed, should yield half a million profit a year over and above a director's salary."

The commissaris coughed as if he had said too much. His eyes strayed back to the balcony. De Gier had replaced the plants that had been either torn or swept right out by the gale. A profusion of begonias covered the balcony's cast-iron railing and their top leaves shimmered in the moonlight like small, succulent, live coins.

"Another brandy sir?"

"Just a nip, a small nip. I must really be on my way"

The crystal decanter appeared once more, and the commissaris sniffed the fragrance of the thick liquid pouring into his glass.

"Your health, sergeant Yes, the baboon was worth

meeting. We won't meet him again. He was sucked into the case by a lonely woman's desires, a woman he might not have liked very much once he got to know her too well. I didn't like Elaine Carnet either. Fortunately I didn't have to, she was dead when we began. Bergen was worse. I should have liked him for he needed our help, but I couldn't make the effort. A fool, sergeant, of the worst variety." He looked into his glass. "Perhaps because he lived on the surface, doing what he thought was proper, following the stream without ever bothering to consider where it was taking him. Well . . ."

"Has Mr. Pullini gone back to Italy, sir?"

The commissaris brightened up again. "Oh, yes, I took him to the airport this morning, after we had breakfast in the Pulitzer, a very enjoyable breakfast. You haven't met him, sergeant, have you?"

"No, sir."

"Pity. A dangerous man in a way but good to be with. We had a marvelous time in his hometown together. Papa Pullini visited Francesco in jail last night. Francesco isn't comfortable but he is reasonably contented. Nobody in Italy should ever find out what happened to him here. He is supposed to have gone on an extended business trip and will be back at the end of the year."

"He will only get a few months, sir?"

The commissaris nodded. "Yes, the prosecutor wasn't too impressed with our charges, fortunately. The charges will stick, of course, they are well documented. Mr. de Bree's statement, Gabrielle's statement, Francesco's own confession, Cardozo's report about the cigars. The defense hasn't got a chance, but even so, just a few months, I would say, and we'll be able to escort Francesco to the airport before the year is over. A beautiful case in a way, a text-book example of provoked manslaughter. It will probably be known as 'the Italian furniture dealer's case' and will be used in examinations."

"And Dr. Havink, sir?"

"Dr. Havink? I thought you would ask me about Mr. de Bree. I would think that de Bree's crime was worse than

Dr. Havink's. I find it very difficult to feel compassion for a man who tries to kill an animal by poisoning. But he did it out of love for another animal, our good friend Tobias. Interesting, very. I hope the judge will probe the case deeply and I'll be in the court listening. Yes, that would be most interesting. I hope he'll get that elderly female judge, she has a brilliant mind.''

"I would like to hear more about Dr. Havink, sir," de Gier said slowly. "I read your reports, but you didn't waste too many words and you made the arrest on your own."

The commissaris drained the rest of his brandy and smacked his lips. De Gier reached for the flask. "No, sergeant, very kind of you, but no more. Well, what can I tell you? A greedy man. It's amazing that medical specialists with high incomes can be that greedy and also that stupid. They can't see their own motivation in spite of all the intelligence they are undoubtedly equipped with. He told me that he practiced his little tricks because he had to pay for his equipment, all that computerized electronic gear he needs for his brain tests. He assured me that the equipment was benefiting humanity. Nonsense. The city doesn't need Dr. Havink's gadgets, our hospitals are overequipped already, and our crippling taxes are partly due to our paranoid fear of death. Why should we have private clinics where already available equipment is duplicated?''

"Yes, sir, but how did you get him?"

The commissaris waved at the begonias. "Ah, the good doctor was so easy to trap. I couldn't use Bergen's skull anymore, it was too badly damaged, so I used my own. I have a friend who is a neurologist and I asked him to arrange for an X-ray of my head. Easy as pie, sergeant, easy as pie. My skull showed no calcifications. Oh, sure, it showed some, but nothing abnormal. Nothing behind which a nasty little tumor could hide. Then I went to Dr. Havink, who had never met me, and registered as a patient suffering from intolerable and chronic headaches. He hemmed and hawed and told me that he would need to photograph my skull. Very well. He did and showed me the photograph. Sure enough, a white spot. And the whole rigamarole about the tumor. Of course it might be nothing, and if it was something it might be harmless, but still, one never knows. Better to be on the safe side. Surely. So would I undergo further tests? Yes, yes, yes. Please. The results of the tests were negative and I was sent on my way again. No mention of money, for I had told him I worked for the municipality and had given him my insurance policy's number. No trouble there.''

"And then you asked him for the photograph with the white spot?''

"Yes. And I whipped it off his desk and ran off with it. He was shouting at me, but by that time I was out the door. My neurologist friend compared the two photographs, which were altogether different, of course.''

"Falsification and embezzlement.''

"Yes, sergeant. And I went back the next day to arrest him. You read my charges, I'm throwing everything at him. He, and some of his colleagues, are manipulating the ignorant by playing on their fears. An old game of the medical profession, it's been with us since the first medicine man went into his trance. They used to charge two pigs and a goat. Now they clean out the insurance companies and the insurance companies grin and raise their premiums. A very old game, sergeant. Cardozo! Rise and shine.''

De Gier telephoned for a taxi, which arrived within minutes, and walked his guests to the elevator.

Grijpstra was on the balcony when de Gier came back.

"Closed,'' de Gier said as he began to gather the debris of the little party.

"What? The bar?''

"Never. No, the Carnet case.''

"I'll have a brandy. I saw where you hid that decanter, there's still a good deal left.''

"But, of course. But first you can help me wash up and I'll vacuum this room. Cardozo has been sitting on his cheese and crackers and you must have walked that sausage into the carpet.''

"You know,'' Grijpstra said half an hour later when the

decanter had appeared again, "that case will still give us a lot of work. Paper shifting. Court sessions. The bloody thing has managed to split itself into three and Bergen's suicide is another inquiry. We'll be running about like ants."

De Gier looked at Grijpstra through the top of his glass. "Yes. And we'll probably be having our skulls photographed. I think the commissaris is all set to attack the doctors, that'll be fun. I wonder how many X-rays my head can stand."

Grijpstra had taken off his jacket and was loosening his tie. "Perhaps. The commissaris seemed very pleased with himself, but I hope the Havink business didn't go the way he described it. He was provoking the doctor, and the judge will throw the case out of court."

De Gier sat up. "Hey. You aren't planning to stay here, are you?"

"Of course. I'm drunk. I'll sleep in that nice big bed of yours and you can bring out the old sleeping bag. Athletes shouldn't sleep in beds anyway."

De Gier poured the rest of the brandy into his glass. "O.K., stay if you like, as long as you fix breakfast in the morning. It's a strange night, I can't get drunk, I'm as sober as when we started. And the commissaris isn't silly. I think I know exactly what he did. He had another X-ray taken after he had been to see Dr. Havink, by a third neurologist. He won't mention the first photograph in court. He'll say that he really suffered from headaches and that he went to Dr. Havink for a diagnosis and, if possible, treatment. But somehow he became suspicious of Dr. Havink's methods and had the results of the tests checked. That first photograph was only to assure himself that there was nothing wrong with his head to start with. He is clever, our chief ant."

The conversation flowed on in bursts and spurts while they had their showers and coffee. De Gier had arranged his sleeping bag so that he could see Grijpstra's face through the open bedroom door.

"Didn't you think the commissaris was rather callous

about that Bergen fellow?''

Grijpstra was talking to Tabriz, who had jumped on the bed, and de Gier had to ask again.

''No. He didn't like Bergen, why should he? I didn't like him either. But the slob was dealt with correctly. Shit, we took a hell of a risk on that cemetery when we were drawing his fire, especially you with your thousand-guilder weed.''

''I took some home,'' de Gier said. ''It's in a pot on the balcony now. I wonder if it will take; weeds are hard to transplant sometimes, especially rare weeds.''

''Bah. You're a detective, not a botanist. You're getting worse all the time. But Bergen can't complain. The commissaris lost all interest once he was dead, but there isn't much we can do for a corpse, especially in the case of suicide. We can't avenge his own stupidity.''

''So the commissaris didn't like Bergen,'' de Gier said.

''Sure.''

''So there are people he doesn't like.''

Tabriz had put a furry paw into Grijpstra's hand and the adjutant was scratching the cat's chin with the other.

''Sure, sergeant. The commissaris doesn't like fools, certain types of fools. Especially fools who never try. There was a time when he didn't like me and he made my life so hard that I was tempted to ask for a transfer, but that is a little while back now.''

''You didn't ask for a transfer, what happened?''

''I started trying again.''

Grijpstra switched the light in the bedroom off. They woke up a few hours later with a start.

''What was that?'' Grijpstra asked sleepily.

''Tabriz. She has got at the marmalade jar again. It broke and there'll be a mess on the kitchen floor. You better watch your step tomorrow or you'll have ten bleeding toes.''

''Why does she do it?''

But de Gier had sunk away again, far beyond the boundaries of his sleeping bag, which curved on the living room floor like a gigantic banana.

''Why?'' Grijpstra asked the ceiling. ''Why, why, why?

There'll never be an end to it, and even when you find the answers they invariably lead to more questions."

He sighed. Tabriz came out of the kitchen, jumped over the sleeping bag, and leaped onto the bed. Grijpstra's hand reached out and the cat put her paw into it. It was sticky.

"Yagh," Grijpstra said.